Chasing Dreams

on

Oak Tree Lane

Oak Tree Lane

Book One

R. A. Hutchins

Cover Design by DMeacham Design

ISBN: 9798875537318

For all those who are chasing their own dreams xx

CONTENTS

Chapter One   1

Chapter Two   13

Chapter Three   21

Chapter Four   29

Chapter Five   36

Chapter Six   44

Chapter Seven   51

Chapter Eight   61

Chapter Nine   69

Chapter Ten   76

Chapter Eleven   86

Chapter Twelve   93

Chapter Thirteen   103

Chapter Fourteen   110

Chapter Fifteen   120

Chapter Sixteen   128

Chapter Seventeen   136

Chapter Eighteen   143

Chapter Nineteen   151

Chapter Twenty   159

Chapter Twenty-One   169

Chapter Twenty -Two   177

Chapter Twenty-Three   185

Chapter Twenty -Four   190

Epilogue   197

Making Memories On Oak Tree Lane   207

About The Author   209

Other Romance books by this Author   211

Excerpt from *To Catch a Feather*   213

ONE

This was not the way it was meant to begin.

They should have been here together, cleaning the place and deciding where to put everything, full of the excitement of starting a new chapter.

As it was, Meg stood alone and, she had to admit, rather forlorn on the main street of the little village she had chosen as her new home, water dripping from the sponge in her hand as she took a moment to catch her breath and take in her new surroundings. Washing windows this filthy was hard work. Not for the first time since she had arrived four days ago, Meg questioned her life choices. What had once been a shared dream had, when it actually became within reach, swiftly become a sole desire and yet Meg had stubbornly held onto it, ploughing ahead with their plans in the hope that he would change his mind. She had arranged the finances herself, offering the bank her inheritance and savings as downpayment to get a mortgage on the old place, convincing herself he could pay her half back when he came around to the idea.

The idea they had talked about for the past six years.

The idea she had made several trips to Lower and Upper Oakley to dream about and flesh out in the hope of catching a property before it was put up for sale to the public.

The idea that he then refused to even discuss.

The further Meg went with the project the further apart they grew, until the point of no return – moving day. Her notice period worked, her boxes packed, the frames and canvases out of storage and snuggly cocooned in bubble wrap, the van scheduled to arrive at any minute, and yet not a single item of his had been moved from its usual place in their shared flat. Then and only then did it really sink in.

She was doing this alone.

Again not for the first time since arriving, Meg wiped a stray tear from her cheek and straightened her protesting back, taking in her surroundings.

What Lower Oakley lacked in size it made up for in charm and location. Perfectly situated at the bottom of Oak Hill, the village was bordered on one side by beautiful fields which rose in a sharp incline to Cheen Castle and the twin village of Upper Oakley, and at the bottom by the North sea, where a small harbour protected a tiny fleet of fishing boats. Lower Oakley had only one main shopping street, Oak Tree Lane, from which all of the residential roads branched off. The whole area was named after the giant, centuries-old oak which stood proudly halfway between its two namesakes. Meg had visited this area often as a girl on holiday with her aunt and had developed what could only be described as a strong affection for the mighty tree, reading into it all kinds of life lessons, such as resilience and endurance. More than that though, the whole place made her heart happy, hence the fact she had just signed away her life savings to buy this prime, if somewhat dilapidated, spot on Oak Tree Lane.

The previous occupants had reluctantly left the place to move in with their daughter down south. Well into their eighties, the Scotts had been running their hardware store in the village for over half a century and were well loved by their neighbours. That the shop front had long since fallen into disrepair, and the irony that the inside hadn't seen a lick of paint for years despite the many tins of the product which the couple themselves sold, had all been overlooked by the locals, who always stood by their own. On the one hand, Meg was grateful that the place needed a thorough update, else she wouldn't have been able to afford it on her own, but on the other the sheer amount of work which now awaited her was thoroughly overwhelming – hence the window cleaning. Baby steps.

Brought out of her thoughts by a shrill shriek behind her and an immediate and rather harrowing wailing, Meg spun around to find a small girl on her knees on the pavement, the water from Meg's now overturned bucket spilling out around her.

"Billy's dead!" The child shrieked, causing not a small amount of alarm to swell in Meg's chest. *How long had she tuned out for? And who on earth was Billy?*

"I, ah, shall I help you up?" Meg bent down beside the chubby infant, realising from this closer vantage point that the little girl must be no more than four or so, judging by the ages of the children who had come to her after-school art club in Durham. That was the extent of Meg's knowledge of little people, however, and when the child's wailing increased with her words rather than subduing to a less ear-splitting level, Meg had to admit she was at a loss. Her own knees were wet now as she ineffectually rubbed the tiny girl's back.

"Leave her, I'll see to her," it was more a growl than a clear command, but it had the effect of sending Meg jumping to her feet and several steps backward. Shielding her eyes from the midday sun, she squinted up at a behemoth of a man, complete with thick stubble and unruly blonde curls. The stranger himself sent a piercing glare Meg's way as he lowered himself onto his haunches, well above the puddle, and lifted the little girl into his arms before balancing her on a strong thigh.

"There, there sweetheart, it's just a bucket and some water, no need to be upset." As if the words were a magical incantation, the child's cries slowed, her face buried in the man's broad chest as he rubbed soothing circles onto her back.

Meg didn't know where to put herself or what to say. She felt like the outsider that she was and so hopped from one foot to the other, wringing her hands. If she was honest, she could really do with someone to rub soothing circles onto her own back, especially someone with big hands like that…

As if just remembering the unfortunate Billy, the infant jerked her head back to look at the man cradling her and through a series of hiccups and sniffles she whispered, "Daddy, Billy's dead."

"No he's not honey, he's just wet," the man soothed, pointing to a drowned-looking bear that was half hidden by the bucket which had clearly fallen on top of the toy.

"Oh, let me get that," Meg jumped to action, happy to have a job to occupy her, "I'm so sorry about the bucket, I…"

"Well you ought to be," the man bit back, standing to tower above her now with the little girl in his arms, his forehead bunched into frown lines, "leaving obstacles in the street like that."

Meg was about to retort with a strong argument in her defence, mainly focusing on the fact that it was a public path and where else was she to put her bucket when she was washing the front windows of the shop, when she noticed that trickles of blood were running down the little girl's legs below the hem of her flowery sundress. Following her gaze the man's eyes widened and his mouth opened as if to speak, but Meg got there first.

"Oh no, you've scraped yourself," Meg directed her words to the child, smiling gently and completely ignoring the father, "why don't we go inside where we can get you cleaned up? And we can get Billy sorted too, I promise, I'll get him as good as new. And there's biscuits," she added for good measure. She was acting on impulse and Meg really had no idea why she'd invited them in, other than she felt a responsibility for the child's injuries. Under any other circumstances, she would have turned her back on the bad mannered bloke and left him to his own apparent dissatisfaction with the world.

"There's really no need, I'll…" the man began quickly, only to be quietened by his daughter who squirmed to be put down.

"Thank you, Billy would like that," she nodded decisively like a tiny grown up, her blonde curls bobbing as Meg lifted the bucket and picked up the soggy bear that had borne the brunt of the watery episode.

Apparently where the daughter went, the man thankfully followed without further objection, only a large sigh escaping him as he trailed after the pair into the cool darkness of the shop.

When the blood had been gently wiped away, with the girl sitting on her dad's knee and Meg dabbing with a damp, clean cotton wool pad of the sort she normally used for make-up removal, it revealed only a small amount of tiny scratches. The little one milked the event for all it was worth, of course, needing a glass of apple juice and two chocolate digestives in order to sit through the whole ordeal and then a bourbon cream to endure the application of a plaster to each of the injured knees. Meg smiled as she finished the task, and tried to shove her long, unruly hair back under the old headscarf she had put on in haste that morning. If she hadn't already found the man to be incredibly disagreeable she might even have considered the small uptick in the side of his face as his stroked his daughter's hair an actual suppressed smile. As it was, the expression was so fleeting Meg couldn't be sure she had even seen it.

Small village and small child aside, Meg was not in the habit of inviting strangers into her space however safe the situation may appear to be and so had left the shop door wide open and declined from inviting the pair up to her home in the flat above. The father and daughter duo were therefore perched on the sole wooden chair in the space, the latter on her dad's lap, surrounded by boxes and bubble wrap which to be honest Meg hadn't had the heart to begin unpacking. The antique chair itself had been left by the shop's previous owners, and Meg wasn't convinced it could support the weight of the huge stranger for very long. Nevertheless, she had tended the child slowly and gently, distracting her by making silly faces and jokes. The man had remained stoic, other than that one, blink-and-you'll-miss-it slip towards the end.

"Now Billy!" The girl shouted, jumping from her father's knee happily as if the whole incident had not occurred and spraying biscuit crumbs onto Meg's head, where she still knelt by the chair. It was an uncomfortable position, to be sure, especially as Meg was determined not to catch the man's eye every time she looked up at his daughter. More than once she had felt his harsh stare boring into her as she worked and had been tempted to match him, glare for glare, but had refrained in the interests of getting this over with as civilly as possible and the rude stranger out of her space. He hadn't even introduced himself for goodness' sake! Talk about bad manners.

"Now Betsie, we can deal with Billy Bear ourselves at home, we need to be getting back now, I've work to do," the bloke said, bending down to retrieve the sodden animal who was still balanced on and dripping into the now upright bucket.

"No!" The girl began to cry again, "I want Aunt Jenna, I want Aunt Jenna…"

"Jenna is still tidying up at Little Acorns," the man said softly – with his daughter at least, Meg noted, he seemed to have unlimited amounts of patience, "you'll see her at nursery again tomorrow morning."

If it surprised her that the girl cried for an aunt and not her mother, Meg didn't let it show in her expression, simply crouching down beside the child once again. The tear-stained face, the tightly balled, tiny fists and the wild curls that had long since come loose from her ponytail tugged at a place deep in Meg's chest. The place that had always held the hope that this new beginning would finally persuade Chris it was time to start a family.

Feeling her own tears threatening, and having to talk around the lump in her throat, Meg spoke calmly and softly, "Betsie, you really do have to do what Daddy tells you, but if you would like to leave Billy here with me then I can have him washed and dried back to his old self by tomorrow. My name's Meg and I promise to take very good care of him."

"Only one night," the girl said morosely.

"Yes, I'll just have him for one…"

"What she means," the guy barked, "is that she only has the bear for one night, then it will be passed on to tomorrow's Star of the Day at preschool to take home."

"Oh! Well, if I put him in the washing machine now he'll dry quickly out in the back yard in this weather and then I could drop him off to you," again Meg spoke placatingly directly to the girl, ignoring the father who waited impatiently in the doorway.

"Yes please," Betsie replied, her wet eyelashes shimmering with unshed tears.

Her father looked like he was about to object, but clearly thought better of it and, no doubt seeing this as the only way he was going to persuade his daughter to leave – especially since she was now eying up the packet of chocolate digestives once again – he nodded brusquely, "Very well, we live in Upper Oakley, though, above Pinewood Pictures, do you have a vehicle? It's a long walk up the hill otherwise. We're next to the Royal Oak Inn on Castle View."

The name of the small art gallery struck a chord in Meg's memory, and she swiftly recalled the rude missive she had been sent a few years ago via email in response to a request that the shop stock some of her paintings. Noting that this man had simply given his address as above the shop, she refused to jump to the assumption that he owned the art studio as well – after all, Meg had already noted that his huge hands would be more suited to other pursuits. Bricklaying and the like. Certainly not fine art. Meg wasn't generally a judgemental person, always trying to see the best in everyone in fact, but this man really had not given her much to work with.

Realising she had tuned out again, Meg forced herself to nod and to the child said, "I'll have him there before bedtime."

Shocked when two chubby arms wrapped themselves around her thighs and squeezed, Meg swallowed down her emotion as the girl was scooped up by her father who stalked out, apparently remembering only in the last moment to say a quick word of thanks.

"Well, I never!" Meg said aloud, in response to the sheer discourteousness of the man. Her heart beat faster in her chest as she watched him stride down the street from the safety of her front step, no doubt reacting to the unfriendly encounter. Nothing to do with the unsettling presence of the man himself. No, none at all.

TWO

It was a long time since Josh Carter had let someone get under his skin the way she had and he was in no way proud of his behaviour. Annoyed with himself that he had been so caught up in thinking about his own problems that he had let Betsie run too far ahead, he had taken his self-recrimination out on the stranger. Further compounded by the fact it had taken her to notice that his own child was bleeding… I mean, what kind of father must she think he was? So, he had been unduly rude, he knew, but had apparently been unable to help himself. "Behaving like a bear with a sore thumb again," his mam would often tell him, and Josh was glad she hadn't witnessed his most recent behaviour. She would have had quite the mouthful to say about it, he knew. Yet the stranger had behaved with perfect politeness, not once rising to his ill manners. Her deep blue eyes had flashed more than once though, and Josh had a feeling that if Betsie were not there she would have given him both barrels. *Why did that thought please him?*

Lifting Betsie into the van and strapping her into the car seat, he couldn't get the image of the petite brunette out of his mind. *Was she even five feet tall?* Josh wondered, before chiding himself as he stomped around to the driver's door. What the woman lacked in stature she had made up for in curves, though, and those paint-splattered dungarees had fit her like a glove, not to mention the way her hair was trailing out of that ludicrous psychedelic scarf thing and sticking to the sides of her face... Josh heard himself grunt in annoyance as he started the engine. He hadn't had these thoughts about anyone since Claire, and he wasn't going to start now. It was likely only the sight of someone other than Jenna or his mum tending to Betsie that had triggered the strange tightness in his chest... *Yes, that was it, that must be the reason.* Satisfied, he gave his head one last shake, hoping the kind newcomer hadn't caught him staring.

Josh's spirits sank further as they rounded the top of the hill alongside the castle and trundled down Castle View into the centre of Upper Oakley. The sight of the art gallery that had been in his late wife's family for decades always caused his stomach to lurch and a heavy melancholy to settle over him. He tried to force a smile as he unclipped Betsie and lifted her out of the van, but his young daughter was too astute, too attuned to his emotions to be fooled. After all, it had only been the two of them for as long as she could remember.

"Sad for Billy?" She asked, rubbing her own nose and sniffling.

"What? Oh, yes sweetheart, but he's in good hands. Would you like to watch some Paw Patrol while I finish up the cabinet for Mrs. Donaldson?"

"No work Daddy, let's play in the garden."

Josh felt the strong pang of guilt that was a regular feature of daily life. The tug of emotions between wanting to spend time with his daughter – to be both mother and father to her – whilst also needing to make ends meet. He could just sell the gallery, he knew, and the apartment above where they lived, and buy somewhere more fit for purpose for his fledgling business, but he hadn't been able to bring himself to do it despite having estate agents round to value the place twice. It still felt like a betrayal of Claire and everything she had loved, even though Josh was still angry with her.

Emotions, messy things, he always concluded. Nor, though, could he muster any enthusiasm for working in the gallery day in day out and trying to sell the few pictures they still had displayed. So, Josh employed a neighbour to open Pinewood Pictures in the mornings whilst he worked on his few commissions in the garden shed. Then in the afternoons, when Betsie was home from Little Acorns Preschool and after some playtime and lunch, he would do what he could on his pieces with Betsie sitting in a camping chair beside him watching cartoons on his laptop. Far from ideal and certainly not a long term solution.

Josh found it hard to refuse his own daughter and so the afternoon proceeded in the usual way, with half an hour of them both playing in the garden after a lunch of sandwiches and cheese straws, the same amount of time washing her babies in the bathroom sink, a full change of clothes for Betsie who would now be covered in mud and water, a snack of several types of chopped up fruit and normally a biscuit or three, and then a precious hour where she would doze off in the camping chair and he would get to work.

Today, though, Josh couldn't focus. His mind was on the locked up gallery and the fact that Martha had left a note saying there had still been no sales that week, the third week in a row in fact, and barely any browsers either. She wondered if Josh was paying her for nothing and felt bad. He felt bad too, but stubbornly refused to do anything proactive about the situation. Despite his mother's advice, which she rarely sugar coated, to cut his ties with the building and move on – for both his and Betsie's sakes. Despite his sister's gentle words of encouragement that enough was enough. That he was allowed to follow his own dream.

But wasn't that what had started this whole trainwreck of events in the first place? Claire following her own dream of being a world-class rock climber? Dreams were for the irresponsible. Dreams were for... well, the dreamers. And that wasn't him. Not one bit.

Meg locked the driver's door of her clapped out Fiat and walked through the tiny, deserted car park. It was barely a couple of hundred metres from the edge of the gravelled area to the tree itself and she sank down gratefully onto the wooden bench at the single picnic table. It was still warm despite the early evening hour, and Meg was glad of it. She had been rather optimistic, it had turned out, promising to have Billy washed, dried and returned by the bed time of a nursery age child. As it was, the toy smelled lovely but was still decidedly damp. Meg laid him out on the rough wooden table to dry, careful to avoid the splatters of bird poo which decorated the surface.

The only building which stood near here, between the twin villages of Lower and Upper Oakley, was Ye Olde Oak Tree Tavern. Despite its medieval sounding name, the establishment only dated back to the nineteen eighties, and Meg recalled many happy teenage hours spent here with her aunt listening to the regular live bands. This had been their summer holiday destination each year without fail, with Aunt Connie saying, "Why should we go abroad when there's such beauty to be found barely fifty miles from home?" She had been right, of course, though the teenage version of Meg had questioned the decision annually.

The late-twenties Meg surveyed the view now, right down into her new home village and further to the blue coastline, and then up to the impressive Norman castle which stood on top of the hill. Named after the French word for oak, 'chêne,' Cheen Castle was a popular tourist spot on the coastal route between Edinburgh and Newcastle-upon-Tyne. Meg took a deep breath in. Fresh air flooded her lungs and she felt a contentment that had always seemed just out of reach during her life in the city. She had enjoyed teaching art in the community college, of course, but it had not been her dream. Merely a stepping stone. On each visit to The Tree as she had always called it, Meg had placed her splayed palms flat against the wide trunk and said a silent prayer that one day she would move here and run her own art studio, where she could sell paintings – her own and those of other local artists – and run classes.

Prompted to repeat the silent wish now, Meg slung her handbag over her shoulder and wandered down to the oak, performing the familiar ritual with a deep longing in her heart. This time she didn't wish for a gallery though – she had achieved that, well the bare bones of it at least – instead she asked for someone to share her life journey with. She had been with Chris for six years, living together for four, yet there had always been a small niggle in her heart – okay, maybe a rather large niggle – that maybe he wasn't 'the one.' Meg had never voiced this, of course, not even to her best friend Lydia, and had silently chided herself for being too romantic. A spillover from the romcoms she enjoyed reading, no doubt.

"Talking to trees, looking for true love, what a fool," she whispered to herself as she hurried back to the car and drove the rest of the way up the hill to Pinewood Pictures.

THREE

Meg pulled up outside the art gallery, noticing immediately the flaked paint around the windows and on the door. She remembered that this place used to be pristine, a spot she loved to visit on her trips to the area. To be fair it had been several years since her last visit, seeing as how the owner had refused to stock any of her paintings, refused to even take a look in fact. It wasn't so much the refusal which had got Meg's back up, as the rude, blunt way in which it had been delivered in a one-line email. Dashing her hopes with a single sentence.

Well, Meg thought, getting out of the car and wondering where the door to the flat above was, *if this is my competition now, I don't think I need to be worried.*

That was one of the things she had been concerned about, opening another art shop in the Oakley area – albeit one that also provided teaching – that Meg would have to compete with this long-established and highly regarded gallery. As it was, the place seemed rather unloved and also half empty, if a quick glance through the dirty window was to be believed, and Meg actually found herself feeling sad that it wasn't the bright, white and welcoming space she remembered from her youth.

Knocking hesitantly on an equally flaky, black door next to the main gallery window, Meg clutched her handbag to her chest nervously before shoving it back onto her shoulder and wringing her hands anxiously. Why the sudden butterflies she had no idea.

Likely just the thought of meeting Mr. Grumpy again, she told herself. It took several minutes before heavy footsteps could be heard coming down the stairs inside and the door was pulled abruptly open.

"Yes? Oh! It's you!" His cheeks were flushed as if he had been exercising, though his forearms were wet, his shirt sleeves rolled up above his elbows.

Meg tried not to look at the damp blonde hairs which covered taut muscle, feeling her own cheeks heat in the process, "I, ah, I promised to bring Billy," she stuttered, annoyed with her own apologetic sounding voice.

"Well, I've just wrangled Betsie out of the bath and into her pyjamas, so it's perfect timing as she's about to get into bed," the bloke said, clearly tempering his voice to sound more reasonable. He even managed a half-smile, no doubt a strained attempt at politeness.

Distracted by the expression, which immediately softened the harsh lines of his face, Meg had the sudden, uncomfortable feeling that something wasn't quite right… that something was… missing. Following the man's eyeline down to her empty hands, his eyes wide and expectant, it suddenly dawned on her.

"Billy!" Meg managed to tone the shriek down to a hoarse whisper so as not to alert the little girl upstairs.

"You didn't bring him?" he asked.

"No, well, I mean yes, I did, but no, I don't have him," Meg wanted the ground to open up and swallow her, she felt so stupid. She had always been prone to self-recrimination which blew a perceived misdemeanour out of all proportion and the current situation was no different. She looked down at her tatty sandals and felt the tears begin to well up behind her eyes.

Don't cry, don't cry, it's a toy bear for goodness' sake, it'll only take fifteen minutes to get him and get back here, she told herself, but it was no use. The waterworks had started and Meg had no way to stop them.

You've let Betsie down, you've embarrassed yourself, and you can't even get the simplest of things right, Meg continued her internal dialogue in her father's voice. Despite him passing away when she was ten, Meg could still hear the disgust and reproach with which he had always spoken to her. Nothing was ever good enough. Nothing could make up for the fact her mother had died while giving birth to her and that was somehow Meg's fault.

Apparently years of therapy hadn't flicked that switch back to a point where Meg could approach her own mistakes with the same logic and compassion with which she treated others. It hadn't helped that Chris had always called her 'ditsy' and 'clumsy,' often mocking her for the slightest error and insinuating she was too disorganised to ever run her own business. Meg had never once challenged him on it, of course, despite Lydia encouraging her many times over the years to do just that. Her response had always been as it was with her father – scuttle away, head down, to cry in private.

Yet, she wasn't in private right now, and Meg didn't dare look up, already imagining the scorn and disapproval she would see there.

Josh wasn't sure what surprised him the most, the fact that she was here without the bear, or that she was crying about it. Perhaps something had happened en route? A collision maybe. People did tend to drive the hill road like lunatics on speed. Josh spared a quick glance at the woman's car, which seemed rather battered in general but there was no huge dent to indicate a crash. Anyway, whatever the reason for her distress, it tugged on Josh's heartstrings evoking protective feelings which he hadn't experienced in a very long time – not for anyone other than his daughter, that is.

"Come upstairs and you can tell us what happened," Josh spoke as softly as he could, wanting to reach out and rub her arm but forcing his hand to remain by his side, "I can put the kettle on and…"

"I'm so sorry, I really shouldn't be trusted with anything impor…" she whispered, stopping abruptly on a sob. Apparently that small confession was his own undoing, as Josh stepped forwards and opened his arms in a gesture of welcome and reassurance, not giving himself a chance to second think the action. Barely recognising himself in fact.

He caught her shocked gasp as she saw the movement, caught the surprise in her eyes as she slowly looked up at him, her brow furrowed and eyes squinted as if trying to read something into his own gaze which might describe his thoughts or explain the unexpected offer. It was a long three seconds as both looked at the other, before she walked straight into his open embrace, hesitating only a brief moment before laying her head on his chest and wrapping her arms as far around his waist as she could reach.

She was so small that Josh could rest his head on top of hers and he did just that, neither of them moving nor speaking. He had expected it to feel awkward, to want to pull away as fast as he had made the spontaneous gesture. But that wasn't the case. Not at all. Instead he felt calmer and more at peace than he had felt in months. In years perhaps.

"I'm Josh by the way," he whispered, reluctantly lifting his head after he felt he had soaked in her goodness for as long as could be deemed appropriate for two strangers locked in a close hug.

"Meg, but I guess you know that already," she replied, tilting her head back to look at him. She looked as confused as he felt, the tears still wet on her cheeks.

"Daddy stop squashing Meg!"

They jumped apart faster than two teens caught doing something they shouldn't, with Josh shoving his hands in his pockets as they both watched his daughter bumping down the stairs.

"Is Billy ready for bedtime snuggles?" Betsie asked Meg, ignoring the red cheeks and tear stained face to search the latter's hands for the toy in question.

Meg could sense Josh's eyes on her, no doubt wondering how she was going to let his daughter down gently.

"Ah, he is yes," Meg began, "but we stopped for ah, a bedtime story, by the old oak, and Billy was enjoying the view and the breeze so much he asked to have a little snooze on the picnic table there. So I'll just be popping back up…"

"I'll get my keys," Josh said, a hint of humour

detectable in his voice.

"Oh no, there's no need, I have my car and…"

The feeling of his hand's light touch on her arm silenced Meg as she felt the heat radiating from the tiny contact.

"Betsie and I will follow in the van then, so you don't have to make the return journey."

"Oh! Yes, that makes sense, thanks," Meg silently scolded herself for causing the man more bother. No doubt he would think her completely ridiculous, not least because he now understood the reason for her tears was a forgotten stuffed animal.

Betsie shrieked with excitement at the unexpected trip out which would delay her bedtime and allowed her father to bundle her up in her dressing gown and slippers before all three hurried out the door with Meg silently praying the bear would be exactly where she had left it.

FOUR

Of course, Billy was waiting there on the table, in the
very same spot where Meg had left him and no worse
for wear after his prolonged visit to the old oak which
gave the area its name. Meg herself let out a quiet sigh
of relief as she watched the little girl skipping ahead of
them to retrieve the toy. The beauty of the place at this
time of day was not lost on her, with the sun low in the
sky and painting it in hues of yellow and orange. The
artist in her wished she had brought a sketch book to
quickly capture the scene, complete with the little
blonde girl who looked like an angel in this light.
Maybe she would even include the tall man who
walked beside her, whose presence Meg felt without
looking. She felt alive in a way she hadn't in a long

time – a certain electricity in her veins which spoke of hope and desire – no doubt from that rather ill-advised hug they had shared, Meg mused silently.

I'm not long out of a long-term relationship, she told herself, *I can't fall head over heels for the first man to show me any kind of common and garden affection. Especially one whose moods seem to change with the wind.*

"I'm sorry you had to come out," Meg paused to look up at Josh, almost afraid to make eye contact in case he saw the effect his close proximity was having on her. The fact she could sense her whole face flushing from the neck up was bad enough, yet she'd felt compelled to break the silence that wove between them like a silken thread.

Perhaps if he gives me a few of his grunted replies and harsh glares like he did earlier in the shop my hormones will get the message, Meg told herself as an excuse to draw the man into conversation.

"Don't be, it's a beautiful evening and there was no harm done. You've done me a favour actually, we're meant to put a picture or drawing in the little diary that comes home with Billy, so that his adventures can be shared with the nursery class the next day. I, ah, always forget and then struggle the next morning to think of a quick activity we can include him in.

Generally it ends up being something messy like baking or fingerpaints," he scrunched his nose up in a way that brought a smile to Meg's lips, "so, ah, now I can take a photo of them both here by the tree, print it out at home and job's a good'un."

Despite her desire that the man's words would have the opposite effect, Meg found herself smiling widely now at the phrase her aunt used to also use for a completed task well done. She caught Josh's eye as he looked her fully in the face for the first time since they'd arrived at the countryside spot and was taken aback by the warmth she saw there. Gone was the Mr. Icy of earlier in the day, to be replaced by this much less abrasive version who was even opening up about his own struggles.

Oh drat, Meg told herself, *the sooner I make my excuses and head home the better.* The fact that the unwanted attraction might be mutual didn't even bear thinking about. Besides, it couldn't possibly be true. Meg forced herself to recall the past years she had wasted trying to convince herself of someone else's feelings, forcing herself to believe that they shared her dreams and plans for the future despite all evidence to the contrary. She certainly didn't want to jump back into the same cycle now with someone she'd just met.

"You have a beautiful smile," Josh whispered, breaking into her thoughts. He even lifted his hand as if he was about to stroke Meg's cheek before apparently realising what he had said and dropping the limb as if it were a hot coal. Meg struggled to hide her shock, feeling her cheeks flush for a completely different reason now as Josh hurried off after his daughter, mumbling quietly to himself. Meg held her hand to her cheek like a fool, watching him go before slowly making her way to the tree to join the pair.

Josh really wasn't sure what had come over him tonight.

I was actually going to stroke her cheek! He muttered to himself as he hurried towards Betsie. Perhaps it had been the military thriller he was currently reading, which had a romantic subplot that he normally tended to avoid. Perhaps it had been the call earlier in the week from his best friend from high school, telling him that not only was he engaged but that the wedding would be in less than two months back home here in Oakley. Yes, that must be it. Too much talk of love, it was making him want things he had no business wanting. Betsie was his future, and hopefully building his business too, if the carpentry gods were smiling down on him for once.

"Daddy, listen!" Betsie rarely did anything quietly, but particularly at this time of day when she was often overtired and overstimulated. Now was no different as Josh watched his daughter bouncing up and down like a kangaroo, waving poor Billy above her head like a flag and pointing with the other hand to the tavern on the other side of the field. Sure enough, when he listened past the small breeze which ruffled the long grass and fluttered the oak leaves, Josh could hear the dulcet tones of his sister Jenna as she warmed up her voice at the microphone in the Olde Oak Tree pub.

"It's Auntie Jenna!" Betsie exclaimed impatiently without waiting for Josh to reply.

"I, ah, thought your sister was the preschool teacher?" Meg asked, perplexed, before realising how silly she must sound – of course the man could have more than one sister! *But surely not two with the same name?* Perhaps the fresh air was going to her head. For sure, Meg felt lightheaded as she watched the man pick his daughter up and swing her round in a circle. Meg had to turn away to hide the tears that sprang to her eyes at the heartwarming sight, the little girl's squeals of delight filling the air. Not once had her own father even held her in an awkward one-armed embrace, let alone played so spontaneously.

"No, she is," Josh smiled, his voice breathless as he set Betsie back down and wiped his brow on his sleeve, his tone far from the pitying, condescending manner her ex would've used at an apparently stupid question, "but she's also part of a 1940s tribute group called The Oakettes. There are four of them and they like to be known as 'vintage vocalists.' Josh shook his head as if the title sounded pretentious to him, but his eyes sparkled with warmth and humour, and Meg could tell from even that small piece of information that he was close to his sister.

"I think I might have heard them once when I came with Aunt Connie," Meg had fond memories of the day, "at the wartime revival fayre that's held by the tree here once a year. 'We'll Meet Again' is it called?"

"Yes, exactly, and they travel round the area doing festivals and weddings sometimes…"

"Let's go listen, Daddy please!" Betsie was now hanging off Josh's arm, still jumping up and down and clutching Billy to her chest with her other hand.

"What have we said about interrupting grown-ups?" Josh asked gently, patting the girl's nose affectionately.

When he thought about it later that evening, alone in bed, Josh would still be none the wiser as to why he had not only agreed immediately to his daughter's request but then proceeded to invite the woman he had only met that morning to join them. The fact that her acceptance of the invitation – albeit with a look of wide surprise – had brought a warmth to his stomach was something Josh refused to dwell on, even in these private moments. His reluctance to say goodbye later in the evening, not knowing when he would see Meg again, was another moment he had no intention of revisiting in his thoughts.

She lives in Lower Oakley, for goodness' sake, he told himself, *I'll probably bump into her again before the week is over!*

FIVE

Meg decided to treat herself to a cooked breakfast the next morning at the Acorn and Squirrel tearoom which was diagonally opposite her own shop on Oak Tree Lane. Unsure whether it was the later night than she'd planned, the small glass of cider, or the close proximity of a certain man all evening that had had her tossing and turning all night, the effect was the same and resulted in a very tired painter this morning. Assuring herself that some good carbohydrates and protein to set her up for the day would do the trick, Meg took the window table at the familiar café and waited for the owner, Janet, to come to take her order.

This tearoom had been here for as long as Meg and Aunt Connie had been visiting the area, though they would normally come for lunch or tea and not breakfast as the latter was provided at the B&B where they always stayed, 'Branches and Blossom,' just a few doors down the street. She took the moment of quiet to survey the small place which was exactly as you would imagine a tearoom in a small Northumberland village to be and which had barely changed over the years that Meg had been visiting. The same faded cotton, Union Jack bunting hung at the windows, the same bleached white tablecloths adorned the few mismatched wooden tables, and the same vintage crockery sat on the shelf which ran the full length of the room on the far wall. Crockery which Meg knew was used only for regulars who could be trusted with its delicate finery, tourists being given the cheap, modern Ikea set that resided hidden under the counter.

Meg had held a soft spot for the woman who had been the first to welcome her back to the village this week – for good this time – ever since Janet had sent a condolence card two years ago when Aunt Connie had been taken by the cancer which had gnawed at her for almost a decade. The gesture had meant a lot to Meg in her grief and had helped to cement the notion that Lower Oakley would be the location of choice for her art studio, whenever it may happen. Ironically it had been the inheritance from her aunt which had formed a large part of the financial package which had finally allowed Meg to follow her dream. There had been so many times when she and Aunt Connie had sat at this very table in fact, discussing Meg's plans for the future, with the woman who had always been like a mother to her jotting the ideas down on a paper napkin to revisit on the train home. Meg had often wondered how her aunt could be so different from her brother, Meg's father, truly proving that the old adage 'the apple doesn't fall far from the tree' wasn't applicable in Connie's case. Meg's father had been like her grandfather and grandmother – his parents – both dour, stoic individuals who rarely showed a smile let alone affection. Connie on the other hand, was like a ray of sunshine in Meg's life, a source of inspiration and Meg's only real model of how a healthy relationship should look.

"You deserve it every bit as much as I do," Meg whispered as if her late aunt could hear her as she stared wistfully at her little shop across the road, as yet without official signage.

"What's that dear?" Janet asked, beaming as she stopped at Meg's table. Always with a smile of welcome and a kind word, the woman was undoubtedly the reason why the somewhat shabby eatery had stayed in business all these years. Meg planned to take a leaf out of her book with her own place.

"Oh, just remembering Connie," Meg gave a watery smile back, seeing no need to hide her grief which still crept up at unsuspecting times.

"Lovely woman, she was, do you remember the day she helped me out when I burned the cake for my lad's twenty-fifth birthday?"

"I do, she was a dab hand with a mixing spoon and some icing," Meg enjoyed the fond reminiscence.

"You'll have to meet him one of these days," Janet went on, "especially as he's been lonely the past while. He's only a few years older than you, you know, and he could do with some adult company." The comment was rather pointed and not lost on Meg.

She had never met Janet's family as, unusually for the tradespeople in the village, the tearoom owner didn't live above her shop, preferring instead to stay in the cottage by the harbour which had been in her family for generations. Meg didn't even know if the adult offspring still lived with her. What she did know though, was that the last thing Meg needed right now was to be the unwilling recipient of any local matchmaking, however kind the intention. She therefore had no plans to meet Janet's son in the near future.

"Ah, I'm too busy to be lonely," Meg hoped the soft reply would not be too subtle, "I'm actually looking for a joiner to help me fit out the studio and hang some signage, maybe build a cupboard or two. Do you know anyone local who might be available at short notice?" She tried to change the subject, to no avail.

"Oh, funny you should mention that, my son's actually got his own carpentry business. Never quite manages to get it off the ground as his attention is always stretched too thin, but he's very talented at what he does, 'Bespoak Builds' is the name. Wait here and I'll fetch you his card."

Janet hurried off and Meg let out a small groan. Apparently she was meeting the man sooner than she'd hoped. Well, she did need a joiner, and if he was willing to give her locals' rates then all the better. As long as Janet didn't start pushing them together...

"Here you are love, you give him a call and he'll see you right."

Meg took the offered card, her appetite for a full English breakfast having disappeared somehow.

Josh had just dropped Betsie at nursery and was about to get into the van when his mobile phone rang. Despite not recognising the number, he answered hoping it might be a potential client. It seemed his mam had been giving his new business cards out with every cup of tea lately.

"Hello, Bespoak Builds."

"Oh! Ah hi, you answered fast. I, ah, was just wondering if you have any time this week to give me a quote on some joinery work in my new art shop in Lower Oakley?"

"Meg, is that you?" Josh's heart thumped in his chest as he recognised the voice of the woman he had been thinking about for most of the night.

"Josh?" *Surely not.*

"I'm just down the street outside the preschool. Give me two minutes and I'll be there… if that's ah, convenient?"

"Yes," Meg's high-pitched squeak embarrassed her and she was about to repeat herself when she realised Josh had disconnected the call.

I guess I had already met Janet's son after all, she thought to herself as she re-plaited her hair and smoothed down her overalls, *but do I want to be working alongside him in this small space, even if it is only for a few days? Not that I've much choice now...*

Josh left the van where it was and shoved his phone into his back pocket. No doubt this was his mother's doing, and he'd be having words with her later, but right now he couldn't focus on anything other than the nervous fluttering in his stomach. It wasn't a good sign, of that he was sure, getting affected like this by a woman he was potentially going to be doing work for. Perhaps he should've said he was busy, had too much on to fit her in.

I suppose I still could, Josh mused to himself, though all thoughts of turning the job down fled at the sight of her through the shop window.

With no make-up, a different set of paint-splattered dungarees that looked at least a size too big today, and just finishing a braid in her hair, she was stunning. Finding his body affected in ways he certainly wouldn't be admitting, Josh paused a moment to take in a few lungfuls of fresh air.

SIX

"Oh! Come in, come in," Meg's eyes caught those of
the man on the other side of the window and she
rushed to pull the door open. *How long has he been
watching me?* She wondered self-consciously, stepping
back as Josh bent his head to get through the low
doorway.

"Did Billy make it safely back to Nursery?"

"What? Oh, yes, we had a bit of a fraught morning.
Betsie never wants to give the toy back," worry lines
formed a few wrinkles on his brow.

"Aw I'm sure it'll all be forgotten by now. Children
that age are so resilient, aren't they? I had no idea it

was you by the way, Janet only mentioned it was her son, and I didn't put two and two together…" Meg shrugged and clamped her mouth shut. Going by the frown which now creased his whole forehead, Josh wasn't too keen on his mother promoting his business either. Or maybe it was just that it had been promoted to her in particular? Meg wasn't sure how she felt about that – *should she want him to want to spend time with her?*

The space certainly seemed a whole lot smaller with him in it and Meg found herself staring at Josh's chest which was the part of him directly in her eyeline. What was once a black t-shirt was now decidedly grey and pulled taught across hidden muscle. She swallowed loudly.

"Well, there's lots of work needs doing and I'd be grateful for a quote for the whole lot and also for each area separately. I'm not sure if I can afford to have everything done in one fell swoop, if you know what I mean. Um, we could go upstairs and discuss it over a cuppa, if you like?" Meg suggested to fill the awkward silence, forcing her eyes to meet his and determined to turn his frown upside down and back once again to the smile that she remembered from last night, "I've unpacked up there and there's somewhere to sit at least."

"No! No, ah," *why had that come out as a croak?* "No, best we stay down here so I can measure up and see exactly what needs doing." Josh took his phone out of his pocket with what he hoped was a purely business-like manner. In the absence of a notebook and pen it would have to do for now.

"Yes, of course, that's more sensible," Meg noted that brash, moody Josh was back to stay and decided she was happy to go along with it. She didn't have the headspace for the feelings that happy, easy-going Josh produced anyway, "I hope you didn't have any appointments you're missing. I'm sorry if I've jumped the queue, I'd be happy to wait for a space…" *I really must stop apologising…*

"I wouldn't have come if I had," That was a lie and Josh knew it, turning away to hide his blushing cheeks from her view.

"Well, I'm glad you could fit me in, at least you don't work in that art shop you live above. You must've met the owner – really rude chap. At first I had my qualms about going into business in competition with his, but if he treats everyone the way he treated me, then I'm pretty sure he can't have many clients left… Oh no, he's not your landlord, is he?" *When would she start to think before she spoke?*

"I, ah," Josh wasn't sure what to say, having no recollection of having met Meg in the past let alone having been rude to her, and definitely not wanting to get into his current circumstances which would involve sharing the details of his wife's death, so he turned to the original wooden counter which still ran the length of the back of the shop, "I guess this is going? Perhaps we could use some of this wood for shelving?"

It was hard to be all about business when she smelled of roses and sunshine, and when she spoke so enthusiastically about her plans for the place. Josh tried hard to focus, adding the specifications to the notes app in his phone and asking appropriate questions when required. Other than that, he followed her about the small place like a puppy, noticing every time her hand brushed against his arm or their thighs met behind the cramped counter. It was far too reminiscent of the previous evening when they had been squashed together on the banquette behind a tiny table in the tavern. It had taken all of Josh's willpower then not to rest a hand on her knee, maybe rubbing his thumb over that joint in a soothing motion, to the point that he had actually encouraged Betsie to swap seats with him, leaving him perched precariously on a low, three-legged stool.

"I had a great time last night," Meg said, as if she could read his mind.

"We'll have to go back when the full quartet are singing, though Jenna and Robyn do sound lovely on their own." *Had that come across like an invitation?* He hoped not.

"They were fab, I enjoyed the more recent covers they did too."

"If you're still interested in asking Matty if you can use the back room at the pub for some art classes, then I can drop you up there on my way back." *Apparently I'm determined to eke out my time with her again.*

"Oh, thanks, but I've got my own car."

"Are you sure that thing's safe?"

Meg felt her hackles rising, "Of course it is!"

"Hmm," Josh didn't sound convinced, and the worry lines were back. Meg much preferred his face without them, "Well, I think I've got everything I need here. I'll get the quote to you in the next couple of days and would be able to start work this time next week if you want to go ahead. Shall I email you the figures, or would it be best to ah, drop in with them?"

"Well, I think it'll be best if I have the numbers in writing, I'll give you my email address," Meg said, her business brain finally clicking in.

"Of course," *Of course she would, she'll be getting a few quotes to compare, you fool! She doesn't want to be put on the spot of having to accept or decline in person.*

It was only then, when he thought about the competition from the two other companies in the area who provided the same services – and on a much larger scale than he ever could, though perhaps not with the same personal touch – that Josh realised how much he wanted this job. Not just for the money. Not even to be doing what he loved. But to show Meg he had what it took as well as to have her admire his woodwork skills. To get the place back to rights alongside her and to soak in her enthusiasm and joy.

So why hadn't he sold himself more? Why had he run hot and cold and all temperatures in between?

"Are you okay?" She was doing that sweet head tilt thing that made him feel like he was the only other person in the universe and that she wanted to know every tiny detail about him.

"Sorry?" Josh tried to clear the frog in his throat.

"You seem a little… off."

"Oh, just thinking about the wood we'd need," he fibbed, "and the children's corner you mentioned. Betsie's going to love that." *Yes, Betsie was a safe topic.*

"Umhm," her bright eyes bored into his, as if she might find the answers shining back at her, "well, I'd love her to help me decorate that area when we get to that stage, with bright handprints and an oak tree made from finger painting."

"She'll love that, thank you."

They both hovered there by the door for a few more seconds, as if the energy crackling in the air around them might persuade one or the other to suggest something else to prolong the interaction. Nothing happened though, except the moment began to feel increasingly charged and awkward, so Josh nodded his head decisively, fumbled his way through another mention of the quotation, and then hurried on his way leaving Meg feeling decidedly off kilter.

SEVEN

The day dragged, with Meg unable to focus on the few jobs she could do around the place before the shelves, units and small counter were installed. There was no point painting, Josh had said, until the bigger fixtures were in place, and Meg didn't have the heart for pulling up the old lino floor today. Besides, it really was a two person task. She could have done some painting up in the flat to start to bring it out of its seventies time funk, or even started a new canvas down by the harbour, of course, but her heart couldn't seem to settle to either activity. She really fancied a shopping spree, buying paints and brushes, water pots and canvases but it all seemed a bit pre-emptive at the moment. Especially since her limited funds needed to go towards getting the place open. All the additional supplies would have to come from another, as yet undecided, pot.

To that end, Meg decided to take Josh's advice and drive up to the Olde Oak tavern to ask the owner Matty if she could use the back room for some art classes. This would hopefully bring in a bit of extra income while the shop was being renovated as well as getting Meg's name and the Brush Stroaks brand out into the local community. Of course, Meg couldn't pass by The Tree without a stop to rest her palms against its gnarly trunk. The wind had risen as the day had progressed, whipping her hair out of the confines of her plait and splaying it across Meg's face. The view was still beautiful, even as she watched summer storm clouds rolling in from the east and even if the gales did drown out the birdsong. Meg paused for a moment to breathe it all in.

Just as she was about to go back to her car and drive the thirty seconds to the car park of the tavern, Meg heard a small squeaking sound rise above the sound of the wind in her ears. There for a second and then gone, she couldn't even be sure she had heard it. Nevertheless, Meg hunted in the tall grass that surrounded the foot of the great oak, stopping periodically to try to hear the sound again.

Perhaps a baby bird has fallen out of its nest, Meg thought, casting a few hopeful glances upwards towards the lower branches but seeing no sign of birdlife this low in the tree. When the creature did finally make a repeat noise it was more of a definite mewl, coming at a lucky moment when the wind died down for a second and Meg was sure the sound was coming from right beside her feet. Sure enough, parting the grass Meg found a tiny patchwork kitten cosied up between two raised roots. There was no mother cat in sight, and despite Meg's efforts to search for it once the baby was snuggled into her fleece-lined raincoat, her hands came up disappointingly empty on that front.

Keen to get the little creature into the warmth of the pub, Meg decided to come back to look for its mother another time, hurrying back to her car with her precious cargo.

The heavy door to the main bar banged open with the force of the wind as the weather almost pushed Meg inside. Glad to get out of the elements, she carried the tiny bundle who was now wrapped in the tartan blanket she kept in the boot of her car.

"Meg! Good to see you again, you're the only one who's ventured out so far this afternoon. Hopefully we'll get some more takers for the pub quiz later," Robyn greeted her with a smile.

Looking around in the daylight, Meg could see just how run down this old place was and wondered how well it was actually doing. Even for the beautiful live singing the other evening, the pub had been barely half full.

"I was hoping to ask your hubby a quick question, if possible, and on the way here I found this little one. You haven't seen a mother cat have you?"

"No sorry we don't have any pets round here, ah she's a cutie," Robyn moved the blanket slightly to get a better look at the tiny face peering out, "and ah, hubby?"

"Your husband, Matty?" Meg could feel the heat rising up her neck and, judging by the look on Robyn's face, she was a long way off the mark as regards the woman's relationship with the pub owner. In her defence, though, Meg knew anyone would've come to the same conclusion having seen the pair messing around and flirting with each other the last time she was here.

"Ah, Matty and I are best friends, 'the' best. I work behind the bar and do the occasional live concert and he gives me lodging upstairs while his dad's setting up his new bar in Portugal. Known each other since we were toddlers. More like a brother really." Now it was Robyn's turn to blush as the sound of someone dropping a heavy box came from the storeroom behind them. A few muttered expletives followed before Matty himself appeared, his eyes looking rather wild. He shot Robyn a look which hinted at a subtext Meg wasn't privy to, and then turned to her.

"Hi Meg, what can I do for you? We don't take in strays I'm afraid."

"Apart from me, eh?" Robyn hip-bumped her boss affectionately before disappearing back the way he had just come.

"I, ah, I" the man seemed lost for words and stood stammering, his man bun wobbling from side to side precariously on top of his head.

"I just came to ask about the back room actually," Meg chose to put him out of his misery, "whether you hire it out for more than family functions? I was thinking about a still life art class, or landscapes… something like that anyway, whatever there's interest in."

"Anything that brings in extra money is a big yes from me," the bar owner smiled and indicated Meg should take a seat at the nearest table, "can I get you anything?"

"Maybe just some milk for this little one," Meg placed the blanket gently on the cushioned bench next to her, opening it slightly and pleased to see that the kitten had stopped shivering.

"Of course, though I'd be taking it to see old Mr. Harris down at Hearts of Oak. He's been the village vet since before I was born and he'll give you the best advice if you're thinking of keeping it."

"Oh! Well, I suppose I could be a foster mother – is that what they call it? Until someone else is found."

Matty didn't look convinced, "Well, this is a small area. Just the two villages, so I wouldn't be holding your breath for any takers." He left to get the milk and Meg picked up the squirming parcel of fur, barely bigger than her cupped palms, and snuggled it against her chest.

"Well Bonnie, I guess it's just the two of us," she whispered, "Aunt Connie would've loved you!"

Luckily this was the one day in the week when the vet's practice stayed open longer in the evening. To balance this, it was closed all day Mondays and a half day on Wednesday afternoon, as is often the way in English villages where all the shops used to close on Wednesday after lunch in times gone by.

Having tipped out a selection of paintbrushes and old rags, Meg had repurposed an old basket as a temporary kitten carrier and was now squashed in the waiting room between two larger ladies, one with a perfectly coiffed poodle and the other with a cat that had been hissing like clockwork every ten seconds since Meg had arrived. Both had said hello as she sat down, but had since kept themselves to themselves, for which Meg was grateful. No doubt her newcomer status would soon wear off and the wary distance that the locals afforded her would disappear with it, leaving her open to their questions and gossip. Such was the goldfish bowl way of things in small villages like this where everybody knew their neighbours' business. Meg wasn't sure how much she was going to like that, having always lived in large cities.

"Mrs. Critton and Polly please," an old, hunched man with a bushy, grey beard emerged from what Meg supposed was the treatment room at the same moment as the bell jangled above the door to indicate a newcomer.

"Meg!" Jenna said, taking the newly vacated seat next to her and trying to encourage an enormous Great Dane to lay down by her feet. Three dog treats, some ear rubs and a stern "down" or five later, the creature finally chose to comply.

"She's beautiful," Meg admired the huge dog, which had black and white markings similar to a dalmatian and the brightest blue eyes Meg had ever seen on an animal.

"Oh thank you. I promised myself I'd get a rescue dog when I had my own place and now was the time."

"Congratulations! Are you in Lower Oakley still?"

"Oh yes, it would take a lot to make me move away from here. And it's not a new house per se, except that my mam has decided to move in above the tearoom which leaves me the cottage. I've tried to persuade her otherwise, mind you, even said I should be the one to live in the flat but she's stubborn! I think she thinks if I have my own place I'll find a man!" Jenna blushed as if having shared too much and Meg smiled.

"Well, at least you've got some gorgeous company anyway. Like me, I planned a solo life and I've just found this little one." They ooh'd and aah'd over the kitten, with Meg keeping it as far from the appreciative eyes of the inquisitive canine as she could until the topic of conversation changed to the previous evening at the tavern, which was when the two women had been introduced by Josh and Betsie.

"I'm so glad you've opened up your art shop in the village and to see Josh smiling and at ease last night… well, I can't remember the last time I've seen him without his tense shoulders up around his ears and his eyes dull and defeated, so thank you. Maybe you can give him some advice on what to do with his own shop, preferably to let it go. It's been a millstone around his neck since Claire died, it was always her dream, her baby, having been passed down from her grandad. She was the painter, Josh was always all about the carpentry, he never had any interest in running an art galler… Oh! Are you okay?"

Meg forced a smile, "Absolutely, just been a really long

day and I think all the moving in has started to take its toll."

"Well if you need any help with the painting or anything, just shout."

Meg nodded her head, her mind whirring as to why Josh would lie to her. Or, to see the best in it, to omit that information when she had directly mentioned the shop. Meg brushed a stray tear from her eye.

She hoped she wasn't allergic to animal fur.

EIGHT

Ten days had passed. Over which time emails had been sent back and forth, styles, prices and timeframes agreed and materials bought. Not once had they met in person, and not once had Meg been anything other than businesslike. She had suggested Josh build what he could in his own workshop – without knowing it was literally a garden shed – and he had gone along with all of her requests as the sooner he finished the job the sooner he would be paid.

They had agreed that a sign should be the first item on the agenda, since Meg was keen for the villagers to know she'd arrived. She had placed flyers for a grand opening, three weeks from now, around the village, on the church noticeboard and in her own shop window

61

and Josh had offered to do the same at Upper Oakley, again omitting the part about his shop ownership. So it was that today was the day they were to put up the small, but rather heavy, square of wood on which Josh had expertly carved the name 'Brush Stroaks.' The rest of the shop front had been painted rather haphazardly on a whim by Meg in the intervening period, and she had decided to go for the 'multi-coloured, paint-splattered, artistic flair' theme which was the opposite of his gallery frontage in Upper Oakley. The staid and conservative façade of that building had stayed the same for decades.

"I love it!" Josh had said when he arrived, and he had meant it. Expecting a smile from the woman who herself never seemed to stop doing so, he had been rewarded instead with a quick "thanks."

Similarly when he had revealed the sign with a flourish, being particularly proud of the palette and brush he had incorporated into the design, she had merely thanked him again. Had Josh not been looking so closely he might have missed the way her eyes lit up at the sight of his work and how she stroked her fingers across the indents of the words when she thought he wasn't looking.

So far, it had been a busy but tense and quiet morning

with both focusing on their own tasks. It had been a
hot week, with today being the hottest day of all, and
Josh was pretty sure he'd heard her gasp when he
removed his t-shirt to work more comfortably. A
sound which matched his own when she went upstairs
to make an iced drink for them both and came back in
the shortest denim shorts he had ever seen. Constantly
aware of her, the hairs on his arms standing on end
when she was close by, Josh chided himself for his
automatic responses. After all, he had sworn off
dreamers – artists in particular – and especially those
selfish enough to forge ahead and do what they
wanted regardless. *I mean, didn't she even tell Robyn in
the pub that first night that she wasn't long out of a
relationship? I bet she dumped him to follow this dream, just
like Betsie and I were left behind...*

The shocking sound of his hammer clattering to the
floor had them both jumping and Josh decided then
and there that it was time for some lunch. On the rare
days that he was contracted to work in the village, his
mam gave him free sausage butties in the tearoom.
Today was even better, as Jenna was keeping Betsie
after preschool and all afternoon for a sleepover that
night with her new Great Dane, so they could 'get to
know each other'. Or some such. As long as the animal
was gentle with Betsie, and so far on their supervised

visits it seemed to be, then Josh was happy. And it gave him a night to himself. A TV dinner for one and an action movie. Oh the freedom!

"Josh!" She sounded rather exasperated.

"Sorry?"

"I said, shall we just put the sign up and call it a day? It's hot and… well, you seem distracted."

"I was just thinking about lunch."

"What is it with men and their stomachs? Let's just put the sign up then the rest of the day is our own. Freedom."

Was that a hint of sarcasm in her voice?

Josh muttered and grumbled, but she was right. It wasn't sensible to do much more heavy work in this heat. Northumberland was only graced with weather like this for about two days out of the year so they might as well enjoy it.

Josh balanced on the top of the ladder, hammer and nails in hand, with Meg holding the bottom of the ladder on the pavement and directing him on whether or not the sign was straight. Focused on her words and trying to move the blasted thing a centimetre to the right, Josh was horrified when the heavy wooden plaque began to slip out of his sweaty grasp.

"Meg!" His shout of warning was too late as the wooden board slid from his wet hands and clipped the front of Meg's brow before landing with a clatter at her feet.

Unable to get down the steps of his ladder fast enough, Josh watched in horror as Meg's body crumpled to the ground.

It had all happened so fast, him falling to his knees and cradling her to him, all the while shouting for help. Derek rushing out of the butcher's and old Mrs. Wattley hobbling out of the baker's as fast as her walking cane would allow, then his mam and her few customers, all crowding round while he phoned 999. Meg coming to and not speaking, just snuggling into his chest as they both sat on the pavement with him feeling helpless, clutching his hand to her head where his mam had given him some tea towels to try to staunch the bleeding.

Josh didn't have the aversion that most people have to

hospitals. Claire had died at the foot of Mount Aconcagua in Argentina. Her body had been repatriated and taken straight to the funeral home. Josh's father, who had left when he was seven and Jenna five, had died three years ago after several strokes, but they had only found out from his obituary in the Newcastle Chronicle, forwarded by mam's sister, Julie. So, no hospital visits there either. Josh had chosen not to go to the funeral, believing that if the man didn't want to see his son in life, then he didn't deserve to in death.

Now though, at the sound of doors swishing, monitors beeping, constant low-level discussion and to top it all that pervasive chemically smell – well, now Josh could understand the almost visceral dislike for the place. Because underpinning all of the sounds and smells, the harsh noises and hard plastic seating, was the fear. The fear that your person wasn't okay. The fear that they might be forever altered. Or, worse still, that you would be walking back through those doors without them. Josh was beginning to understand.

What if her beautiful smile was gone? What if she blamed him? It was his fault, after all. What if, what if, what if?

The paramedic had assured them both that the fact Meg had stayed conscious throughout the journey to the hospital was a positive thing. She had referred to "his wife" and neither Josh nor Meg had corrected her. Josh had the distinct impression Meg was one of those people who hated hospitals, if the way she had clung to his hand and begged him not to take her there was any indication. So, Josh had let the paramedics mislabel him – he would have let them call him anything, in fact, if it meant staying with Meg in that moment and those that followed. In the ambulance, once the professionals had made Meg as comfortable as possible, Josh had shielded her head and torso with his upper body, holding both of her hands in his huge one and leaning over her in the hope of calming her evident panic at their destination. He had stroked her hair back gently with his spare hand, being careful to avoid her wound, and whispered words of apology and reassurance. He hoped he'd done a good job of it, spoken as the assurances were past the huge lump in his throat caused by forcing back the tears that were determined to fall. He wasn't normally a crier. Had been told by his mam and Jenna that he kept things far too bottled up, in fact. So why did he feel like the floodgates were about to open?

It had all happened too quickly once they'd arrived. Her wheeled away to be triaged, him sent to check her in. It was only then that he had realised he didn't even know her surname, so in a moment of panic had given his own. Meg Carter.

"Mr. Carter, you can go in to see your wife now."

He didn't correct that nurse, either.

NINE

Meg hated hospitals.

It was almost hardwired into her genetics, she decided. Having lost her father at ten after an extended hospital stay during which he insisted his daughter visit him daily after school, and now Aunt Connie just a couple of years ago after more hospital appointments and admissions than either of them cared to count, Meg had vowed never to go in another. A silly promise, and one she couldn't possibly keep, she knew, but really it would've had to have been a life or death situation for her to willingly make this choice. Not a simple scratch on her head. Meg tried to remove the monitor that was tracing her heartbeat, causing the machine to protest loudly.

"Hey, what's happening?" Of course, Josh would enter at that very moment, followed by a nurse who pushed past him and hurried straight over to the complaining machine.

His face was white, his hazel eyes wide and searching. They stared at each other wordlessly until the woman nodded silently and left. For a moment, peace reigned and Meg let her eyes flutter shut. She certainly was tired and the infernal heat wasn't helping, maybe just a quick snooze…

"…with this kind of head trauma and suspected concussion we ask that the patient not be left alone for twenty four hours following the incident. Will you be with your wife all evening?" Josh nodded wordlessly at the kindly doctor, "Ah, here she is now. Hello Meg, how are you feeling? Like you've been hit on the head, I bet. Never mind, a few days and you'll be right as rain, just remember to come back next week to have those stitches removed. You're free to go home whenever you're ready." A small pat on her foot which was hidden under the covers and he was gone.

Wife? What had happened while she was asleep? As she

tuned into her surroundings, Meg felt the heaviness of a hand encasing her own. She looked to the limb in question, then followed it back to its source and up to two swollen and bloodshot, wide eyes searching her own. Feeling dizzy with the simple effect of moving her eyes, she closed them again and took her hand back rather roughly.

"Meg, ah," it came out scratchy and he cleared his throat, "ah, I'm so sorry."

"And so you should be! Marrying someone without their consent!"

"What? No! I mean I may have let them believe, and then I didn't have your surname so I had to run with that one on the spur of the moment, but I mean… no, we're not married." She let out an audible sigh of relief, so loud that had Josh himself not been so relieved that she was okay, he might have felt offended, "No, I meant I'm sorry for dropping the sign on you. It was a hot day, my palms were sweaty. I don't have the words to make it all okay."

"Thank goodness, ah , I mean, marriage never really works out, does it? Aunt Connie's marriage lasted all of three years in the eighties before he cheated on her, my relationship lasted six years and he wouldn't even put a ring on it…" Meg clamped her mouth shut lest this verbal diarrhoea continue.

What medication had they given her?

"Meg, I was apologising for the accident, do you remember the sign falling on your head? I feel so awful. Of course I'll stay with you all night like the doctor said. Betsie is with Jenna and mam will keep checking on her too, so I'm all yours."

Meg's eyes flew open at that and Josh really wished he'd worded it differently.

"There's no need," Meg said, yawning, "I'm fine by myself, I don't need…"

"Doctor's orders," Josh said firmly, before more gently adding, "it's the least I can do."

"Well, I only have one bed, and you're the rude man from the art shop in Upper Oakley who refused to stock my paintings, and you kept that select bit of information from me, so maybe I don't want to share my bed with you!" *What was it with the truth serum? Damn, this was strong stuff.*

"Well, first of all I'm not looking to share your bed, Meg. I'm strictly on the sofa. Second, I just didn't want you to have a preconceived idea of me. I wanted you to get to know me properly, that was why I didn't correct your assumptions about the gallery. I don't know, perhaps I was wrong. But you only mentioned it the once, not since, and I've searched your name in my emails, ah…" He raked his hands through his curls, "And I'm sorry for the curt reply I gave you back then. In my defence, my wife had just died and I was struggling to find a new routine with a one year old through my grief, I hadn't even got round to thinking what to do with the shop, so…"

"Betsie lost her mum at one? Oh no, I never knew my mum so I can understand, you see? The only one who ever loved me was Aunt Connie. Not my father. Never him. Not Chris either, I don't think, or maybe he just loved me in the beginning then I made him fall out of love…" Meg couldn't stop the tears which flowed down her face now, "The pair of you though… it's clear how much you love Betsie and it's all so sad, don't worry about a stupid message from years ago." Meg scraped the back of her hand indelicately across her running nose.

Josh wasn't sure what to address first, her distress at his own bereavement, her own childhood loss and feeling she'd lacked love in her life, or the fact that all he wanted to do was console this beautiful woman whose heart was bigger than any he'd ever met. Grabbing a paper tissue from a box on the bedside table he gently wiped her tears, whispering words of consolation.

Meg wasn't used to being taken care of like this. She wasn't sure whether to pull away and reassert her independence, or to lean into it and enjoy it for the brief time it was offered. In the end, the latter won and she found herself resting the side of her cheek, wet as it was, against his and holding him close to her with her palm round the outside of his biceps. If Josh was surprised by the sudden movement, he didn't show it, simply scooting his chair closer and placing the arm that she held onto her back and so holding her to him. His other hand traced the cheek that wasn't glued to his own and he felt each breath she took, each small sigh of contentment. Moments passed before he felt her thumb tracing circles over the muscles on his upper arm. Startled, he mirrored the movement on her back, caught up in the coconut smell of her hair and the softness of her skin against his cheek which managed to override the harshness of their surroundings to invade his senses.

It felt intensely intimate. Despite them both knowing that it was likely a result of her concussion and his guilt they let the embrace last for as long as possible, savouring the feeling of shared breaths and mutual understanding.

If there were ever two lonely souls reaching out to one another it was these two in this moment.

TEN

Trust his sister to own the only classic car this side of the Tyne that had only two seats. Jenna's racing green 1966 MG Roadster convertible – affectionately nicknamed Gloria – was her pride and joy and clearly not suitable for transferring patients to and from the hospital. Especially not with the giant hound who accompanied her on the front seat of the fish and chip van.

"Brin lent me his van," Jenna chirped, "it's got rear seats for you two and he and mam are looking after Betsie at the harbour cottage."

Brin McGovern had been running the fish and chip shop by the pier in Lower Oakley for as long as Josh's mam had been running the tearoom. Never seeing each other as competitors they had formed a companiable friendship over the years, which Josh suspected may have recently turned into something more. May even be the reason Janet wanted to move into the flat above the shop on her own, in fact. He hadn't discussed it with his sister, matters of the heart being off the safe topic of conversation list since Claire died, nor did he intend to. His mother's love life was her own business. It would just be nice if she stopped trying to pry into his.

Love life? That's a joke, he thought sardonically, though he did wish Janet would stop phoning every day to ask if he needed a babysitter so he and Meg could go out. *Well, she got her wish, though probably not the date night she'd intended!*

"It smells of fish!" Meg used her fingers to peg her nose and giggled like a schoolgirl. Josh couldn't help but smile back as he watched Jenna help her with her seatbelt and tuck a blanket around her knees.

"Well, it was the best I could come up with on short notice," Jenna smiled.

"And what about the wolfhound?" Josh asked, nodding towards the slavering creature who watched his sister's every move intently.

"We're, ah, having some separation anxiety issues, aren't we Greta?" Jenna raised an eyebrow and gave a rueful smile, "You might be right about the hound part – if I'm even out of her sight long enough to go to the loo she starts howling like all hell has broken loose. Good job I don't really have any neighbours down by the water, just old Charlie who's almost as deaf as a post anyway."

"Do you feel well enough for us to start moving?" Josh asked Meg gently, "No Nausea or dizziness?"

"Yes, I'm feeling much better for having had some fresh air and that tea and toast you got me before we left." It was true, Meg no longer felt quite like her tongue might run away with her secrets at any moment, and she was glad. Goodness knows what she might have admitted to him otherwise. This gorgeous man with the sad eyes and off limits emotions. That was at least twice now that Meg felt she had found a chink in his armour and broken through his defences.

Meg was happy to look out the window as the siblings chatted about an upcoming wedding, the news of which seemed to have put Jenna a bit out of sorts.

"A couple of months? How will they even get it organised in time?" Jenna's voice had become high-pitched and Meg could see her casting glances at Josh in the rear view mirror.

"Well, you know Simon's parents still live in Upper Oakley so his mum will be all over it like a bee with a honey pot. I think it's a small ceremony in the church and then a reception at The Royal Oak Inn. You know she was always for keeping up appearances, even when we were teenagers."

"Will Nick be there?" The question was whispered so softly that Meg had to strain to hear it.

"Well, we've always been the three amigos so yes, I think he'll be asked to be joint best man with me, though Simon did mention he was having trouble getting hold of him," despite the levity in his voice, Josh's frown lines were back and Meg turned her head to study his side profile fully. The man himself was focused on his sister and her reaction to this news. Whoever this Nick was, Meg concluded, Jenna had no desire to see him again.

"How did he get leave at such short notice?" Jenna's face was pale and the gearbox shrieked as she crunched the manual gear change.

"He's done with the army, or rather the army is done with him. He was medically discharged eight months ago. Simon only found out because he happened to bump into the man in question in Newcastle a few months back, though, I don't think it's public knowledge." Now it was Josh speaking in an almost reverential whisper, "I assumed you knew, thought Tasha would've mentioned it to Mam?"

"No, no I didn't. But he didn't come back to Oakley? Why not? I know Tasha would have him back in a heartbeat. She's trained in holistic therapies for goodness' sake, she must have something up her sleeve to help her son?"

"You'd have to ask him that yourself, I'm pretty sure you and Mam are invited. I think Betsie's a flower girl of all things, you might have to help me get her kitted out for that. The invites should be arriving any day now." Josh said, desperate to stick to the facts and move off the topic as quickly as possible.

Jenna simply shook her head as if she had no intention of making contact with this Nick, lifting one hand off the large wheel to stroke the dog beside her absentmindedly.

Not for the first time Josh wished they didn't live quite so in the middle of nowhere. Everything was at least a half an hour drive away. Big supermarket? Thirty-five minutes. Hospital? Forty minutes if there was no traffic. Airport? You'd be lucky to get there in under an hour.

Jenna seemed to speed up after that, clearly as keen to get back to Lower Oakley as her passengers. The dog started barking when she killed the engine outside Brush Stroaks, no doubt worried that she might be left behind in the van. She needn't have panicked as Jenna dispatched the pair into the building in two minutes flat and disappeared down the street. She was well riled up, Josh knew, and he agreed she had every right to be. Even after all this time and distance. His best friend was the only one his sister had loved and the only one who had ever broken her heart. That wasn't something she would ever forget or forgive – in fact, it had taken Josh himself a long while to do so.

Bringing his attention back to the matter at hand, and the woman he had just followed gingerly up the steep staircase to the tiny apartment, purposefully alert in case she fell backwards, Josh had to admit to feeling a bit strange going into Meg's living space for the first time under these circumstances. He hadn't been here long enough this morning to need to use the bathroom or to take a turn making their drinks, and had the feeling Meg had been as relieved as he was that they were both in the public part of the building.

That wasn't the case any longer, however, and Josh did a double take as he arrived at the top of the stairs which led directly into an open plan sitting room and kitchen. Don't let that description of modern open plan living fool you, though, as this place was anything but!

"Holy mustard sauce Batman, it's like stepping back into the seventies in here!"

Meg smiled widely, "Ah yes, I haven't gotten around to painting this room yet. My friend Lydia is coming from Durham next weekend to help me. I'm not sure, what will go best over lurid brown, orange and mustard patterned wallpaper?"

"Those circles are going to give you a new headache," Josh replied, "but please don't tell me you're getting rid of this thick, brown pile carpet? Think of all the history that's hiding in there!"

"Eugh don't, please, it's enough to give me nightmares," Meg sank down onto the sofa that she'd acquired from a charity shop in Durham before she left. It was cream leather and had cleaned and polished up a treat. Meg felt its coolness on her bare legs now – she still couldn't believe she'd gone to hospital in her workwear-only, not-to-be-seen-in-public shorts that she'd only worn to give Josh a taste of his own medicine. *How was that only this morning?* Little Bonnie had met them at the top of the stairs the moment they arrived and curled up now on Meg's lap. Thankfully, the little kitten slept most of the day anyway, and Meg had already fed her before the impromptu visit to A&E.

"Who's this beauty?" Josh asked softly, reaching down to stroke the cat and so putting his head much closer to Meg's. His large finger traced a line down the kitten's tiny back, careful not to tread father and end up on the smooth skin of Meg's thigh, though the thought seemed to overwhelm him for a moment and his finger hovered in mid-air until he caught himself. Bonnie snuggled further into her owner and Josh straightened up.

"It's Bonnie. A gift from The Tree. Put the kettle on, will you?" She spoke around a yawn, hoping to put a bit of space between them. Not that that would be easy in her tiny flat. Between the kitchenette and sofa there was a little Ikea dining table for two, a small television on an antique side table that she hadn't yet had a chance to sand and polish – another charity shop find – and a large expanse of hideous carpet that had simply sucked up into its murky depths any and all attempts to clean it with soap and water or carpet cleaners.

"I'll make us some food, shall I? It's well past teatime, so we could have some supper?"

"There's pasta and sauce if you like, I'm not too hungry, probably the toast I had," Meg said, remembering the way Josh had eyed the snack longingly in the hospital. It only just dawned on her that he hadn't eaten all day, "Or I could cook for us?"

"You absolutely won't be getting up from that settee. It's my job to look after you tonight," Josh said, before blushing hotly and busying himself in the kitchen.

Meg wasn't sure how she felt. Not just about the pain in her head, but about the one in her heart too. She wasn't looking for a new relationship. She had rarely seen one that had ever succeeded in making both parties happy, after all, and she certainly hadn't experienced one personally. That was six years of her life she'd never get back. But the rest of her body didn't have a concussion, and it thought the idea of a few snuggles with Josh a very good plan. Meg pulled the throw blanket from the back of the sofa and rearranged herself under it and the tiny kitten on top of it, cosied against her chest.

"Since my own defences are low, you'll have to be my

shield, Bonnie," she whispered to the purring cat, as they both stared at the broad back of the man making himself at home in her kitchen.

ELEVEN

"So, how does the tree give you gifts then? I could do with a new work van actually…" Josh worried that Meg's concussion might be getting worse as he handed her a cup of tea. The meal had been bland but, in his opinion, passable and thankfully Meg hadn't complained. Rather than make her walk the few steps to the table, Josh had brought her meal to her on a tray he found in the kitchen cupboard, and then wedged himself beside her on the two-person sofa. It had been cosy, to say the least, and at the first opportunity Josh had jumped up to make them a drink, taking advantage of waiting for the kettle to boil to pop to the bathroom and splash some cold water on his face. Normal Meg was one thing, but completely relaxed

Meg with all her defences down and her complete focus on you was… gorgeous.

"Oh, well I was there with my hands flattened against the trunk, like, you know…" Meg said, her eyes shining as she recalled it, her face nodding to encourage him to recount his own similar experience.

"Um, not sure I do? Do you mean you hug it?" Josh was turned to face her on the settee, deliberately occupying his hands with his drink.

"Yes, sort of, I just get in really close and flatten my hands against the trunk like this," both hands landed flat on his T-shirt clad chest, "and let its energy flow into me as I make a wish." She turned her head away abruptly then as if embarrassed, but seemed to forget to take back her hands.

Josh wanted above anything to keep her talking, for her to continue sharing in this close way that he hadn't experienced with anyone for so long. He put his cup down on the floor and took one of her hands in his, rubbing the palm in what he hoped was encouragement, "So, you put this hand on the trunk… And you wished for a kitten?" Josh hoped any scepticism he had was well hidden.

I mean, she has the evidence to prove it, he thought.

"What? No, silly, I wished for a…" Meg paused and her cheeks reddened further. Josh couldn't help but smile now at how cute she looked, suddenly all flustered, "Well, what I wished for doesn't matter. I got a kitten!"

"So you did," Josh said, dragging his eyes away from hers to look at the small creature who lay snoring by Meg's feet. He really wanted to know what she'd wished for, of course, but sensed that might be a conversation for another time. The shared trauma of the day had forced an intimacy between them, but Josh didn't want to take advantage of that.

Meg clearly shared his opinion, "It's been a long day," she yawned around the words and pulled back. Josh took that as his cue to help her get settled for the night. The kitten, too, appeared to sense the change in atmosphere and skulked over to wait by Meg's bedroom door, no doubt determined that she wasn't going to be left out in the sitting room all night with the strange giant.

"Let me help you to the bathroom," Josh stood and held out both hands.

"I can manage," Meg replied, whilst simultaneously taking his hands in hers and allowing him to help her off the sofa.

The sudden movement made her momentarily dizzy and Meg stumbled forward and into Josh's arms. There was barely any air between their bodies now and Josh was afraid to move. Afraid to touch her the way he wanted to and equally afraid to break the spell by putting some distance between them. Meg, too, seemed to have the same dilemma, tilting her head to the side and looking up at him with a soft, questioning gaze that was almost his undoing.

It was her hands untangling themselves from his so that her arms could come up to loop around Josh's neck that broke the last thread of his restraint and he lowered his head to hers, his hands sliding slowly behind Meg's back as he did so. They hovered there for a moment, their lips still not touching as their breath caressed the other's face. No desire to rush the moment, both of them taking it all in – the feeling of closeness, the sounds of their hushed and shallow breathing.

Until Meg lifted her hands and tangled them in the curls at the back of Josh's head. This simple movement brought his desire rushing forward and he had to force himself at the last moment to cage it, managing to touch her lips softly with his own. Barely a flutter, a hope with the hint of a promise. In keeping with their slow dance of courtship, they rested there for a moment, until Meg pulled back slightly and looked him directly in the eyes again, this time a small smile gracing the lips that his own had just been preparing to caress. She moved as if to rejoin their mouths and Josh was frozen in anticipation, his head bent to hers, when a shrill noise blasted from the kitchen bench.

A tinny version of 'You Are My Sunshine' filled the room, causing the two to jump apart. Josh's blood had all run elsewhere and his sense with it, it seemed, as it took him a good few seconds to register that the noise was coming from his own mobile phone.

"Betsie!" he exclaimed, rushing over to answer, his fingertips ghosting across his lips as if the whole thing may have just been a dream.

Meg took herself off to the bathroom to give Josh some privacy, but had barely shut the door behind her when she heard his voice getting louder as he hurried back across the main living space and tapped gently. She opened it again and waited for the call to finish. Josh seemed to be vibrating with energy and Meg knew the feeling. The adrenaline that had been flowing only moments ago when she had felt safe and cherished in his embrace hadn't yet dissipated.

Josh's hand shook where he held the phone to his ear, "I just shouldn't leave her. That was the one stipulation from the doctor." The frown lines were back in force and Meg wanted to smooth them out with her finger.

Instead, she whispered, "I'll be fine, you go."

"It's Betsie, she's crying for me and Jenna says she has a raised temperature," he held the phone away to speak to Meg directly.

It was clear from his anguished expression that the man was torn and Meg wanted desperately to put him out of his misery, "She needs you, Josh, why don't you go and collect her and bring her here. We'll sort out the sleeping arrangements later. Main thing is that she's with you."

"Are you sure? I hadn't even considered bringing her…"

"Absolutely, now go," Meg pushed his chest with her forefinger as he finished up the call with Jenna.

"I'll sit back on the sofa while you're out. Won't even try to stand," she reassured him when he looked like he might waiver.

"Promise?"

"Promise."

Luckily Josh's van was still outside from earlier in the day, though to Meg it felt like she had lived several days since they had worked on the shop. Curling up on the sofa after a quick toilet visit, and with a thoroughly confused Bonnie, Meg drifted off to sleep.

TWELVE

"Meg! Daddy says we're having a sleepover!"

Meg awoke suddenly with a pounding headache. The short nap had done her more harm than good, as it was a much sounder sleep that her body needed right now. She sat up groggily and accepted the squeezy hug from the little girl in fleece pyjamas who had entered the room like a tornado.

"I'm sorry," Josh mouthed from behind his daughter.

"How are you feeling, poppet?" Meg asked, struggling to focus.

"Much better now I have my daddy," Betsie pulled

back and Meg could see that the girl's cheeks were flushed, marred further by the track marks left behind by drying tears.

"We, ah, haven't been apart much," Josh sat down with Betsie on his lap, keeping his eyes averted from Meg, "this was only her second time trying a sleepover. I should've known, the first one didn't quite go to plan either."

"That time, Daddy came to have a sleepover at Nana's house too!" Betsie said cheerily.

Meg wished Josh would look at her. She hoped he didn't feel embarrassed or worse, ashamed by his daughter needing him. It was completely natural that they would have a close bond after everything they'd been through, and Meg didn't ever want Josh to feel bad for that.

"Of course, it'll be more fun with three anyway," Meg flashed a genuine smile at the little girl, as Josh turned his head and looked directly at her for the first time since getting back. He raised one eyebrow in a questioning gaze, a small smile on his lips that almost dared Meg to consider the potential lie in her statement. To imagine what it might've been like if it had continued being just the two of them. Meg smiled back knowingly and the shared moment seemed to put him back at ease.

"Oh! Is that a baby kitty-cat?" The question was more of a squeal as the girl saw the flash of fur as the kitten tried to hide further under the blanket. An onslaught of chubby hands and gentle guidance followed until Bonnie was curled up on Betsie's lap between the two adults and, to be honest, Meg felt like she had been hit by a bus. The tiredness, the head injury, was all catching up with her.

Looking sideways over his daughter's head, Josh looked at Meg intently, his eyes almost slits as he scrutinised her face. "You look paler than before," he whispered, though there was no need as Betsie was oblivious to their conversation, so engrossed was she in the kitten.

"Tired, head hurts a bit," Meg too spoke in hushed tones.

"Oh goodness, you should have had more painkillers by now, they're on the bench in the kitchen where I left them when we came in," the look of guilt was back and Meg couldn't bear to see it.

"I'm a grown woman, I should've thought myself," she said, attempting to stand.

"No, I'll get them," Josh was faster and Meg happily let him win the race, slumping back down.

"Perhaps we should work out where we'll all sleep," Meg murmured when the tablets were downed with a glass of tepid tap water.

A prolonged, whispered discussion ensued, whereby Josh knelt beside Meg as they debated back and forth with him insisting she have the bed and she determined that her guests should. In the end, the decision was made for them as a moment of stillness in the discussion left space for the sound of gentle snoring beside them. Betsie lay curled on her side, her head resting on a cushion at the other end of the sofa, the kitten curled up beside her, and the blanket over her legs. The proverbial calm after the storm.

"Well, I guess that settles that," Josh said, "You have the bed, I'll lie on the floor beside Betsie."

"Well, I don't have any extra sheets or pillows yet, so that won't work," in truth Meg had no more energy to argue. She was ready to forgo a shower and collapse straight into bed at this point.

"Come on, let's get you settled," Josh said, ignoring the problem, "you're shattered." He checked Betsie was sleeping soundly before helping Meg into the adjoining bedroom.

The last thing Josh wanted was to cause Meg further pain or upset. To be honest, he was past caring where he slept, so exhausted was he. So, he left the door between the two rooms open, turned his back as Meg slipped out of her shorts and into pyjamas, listened to the sounds of her getting into the bed and then turned and moved to join her when she patted the bed beside her, inviting him to lie down. On top of the covers, that is. They were both too tired to feel any awkwardness, and Josh fully intended to be back in the sitting room before Betsie stirred, but he needed a couple of hours sleep, just to recharge. He could hear Betsie from here if she shouted for him, he could listen for Meg stirring if her head pain worsened or she started vomiting. Yes, just a few moments of shut eye...

"Josh?"

"I'm so sorry, I didn't mean to wake you, I was just checking on Betsie to make sure she was under the blanket and I thought to bring in the painkillers and a glass of water to put on your nightstand for when you woke up. I really didn't want to disturb you."

"No matter, what time is it?"

"Ten past five, try to go back to sleep," Josh edged back around to his side of the bed, guilt assailing him when Meg turned to face him instead of drifting back off.

"Are you sure you don't want to come under the covers?" Her voice was thick with sleep and more sultry than he had heard her before. Such a big turn on and despite Josh's body reacting his resolve held firm.

"No, honey, I'm fine on top here," in truth he was pretty cold and uncomfortable, trying to keep to his edge of the bed for propriety's sake even in his sleep, but Josh certainly wouldn't admit to that. The comfort of the two females in the flat was his top priority.

Meg released a slow sigh, of contentment or resignation Josh couldn't tell, and shuffled closer to him, resting her head on his shoulder.

"You're such a good dad, you know?" She whispered, not giving him any chance to reply, "And I should know, I had the opposite and believe me, he set the bar very low. For a long time I thought it was me, that I was the problem, but more recently I've realised that I can't blame little Meg for an adult's reaction to my mere presence. Little Meg did nothing wrong."

Josh didn't dare speak, even quietening his breathing so that Meg would keep opening up to him. He wanted to roll onto his side so he would at least be facing her, but was worried that this might spook her so continued lying on his back, his face only slightly angled to the side. The warmth coming from Meg's body was comforting, and the weight of her head a grounding force. So much so that he unconsciously let himself fully relax for the first time that night, simply listening to her voice which soothed him in ways he couldn't even explain.

"Little Meg just wanted to be loved, yet nothing she tried worked. She learned to be a people pleaser and to hide her emotions deep inside, never wanting to cause trouble and so having no boundaries to protect herself. I know you won't do that with Betsie, you'll give her the confidence to value herself and the wings to fly, to reach her dreams. You should be proud, Josh, being a single parent is no easy ride." She moved her arm so that it was lying across his waist, just above the band of his jeans and Josh welcomed the added closeness.

"I do want her to achieve her dreams, of course," Josh began, haltingly at first and then it was as if a dam had burst as he shared what he had never voiced to any other, "she's my daughter and I would give her the world if I could, or at least help her to grab it with her own two hands. But that bothers me, you see, because I've seen what dreams can do. The selfish pursuit of them. My wife, Claire, died trying to climb one of the hardest peaks, constantly striving to push herself, to test her skills, to prove herself. When her dreams took her away for good and Betsie and I were left alone, I promised I would never let dreams dictate our lives again. But when you speak of Betsie, of course I agree that she should be equipped to live her life to achieve everything she sets her mind on. It's a conundrum which would tear my heart apart if I let myself dwell on it very often."

Without realising it, he had turned so that their bodies were touching, Meg still under the blanket and he atop it. Her arm rested across him still, but their faces were now so close he could make out her features in the semi darkness.

"Well, if that's what's holding you back from pursuing your own dreams, that you think it's selfish and potentially dangerous, then I understand but I'm not sure I agree with you," Meg said gently, speaking slowly so as to choose her words carefully, "would it perhaps be setting a good example to Betsie if you do follow your passions? If she watched you set up a business and thrive in your craft would that be a bad thing? Very few dreams are as extreme as rock climbing, I would guess, and dreams as and of themselves are not necessarily selfish, especially not if they're truly shared by all involved. Would it be selfish to want to provide a better life for you and your child? Absolutely not. What happened to Claire was tragic, just awful, but not every personal endeavour is destined to end in disaster." She moved her hand up to stroke the back of his neck and Josh had to fight back the tears that he had held in check for so long.

"We argued about it so much before she left," he whispered, "I was torn between wanting her to do everything she strove for, and keeping her safe at home with me and Betsie. Maybe I was the selfish one for wanting that?"

"I don't think it's selfish to want to keep your loved ones safe and close," Meg rested her forehead against his, aware from the sniffles he tried to hide that Josh was upset. Her hand soothed his scalp and neck under his curls and her mouth whispered close to his, "I guess it's just a balance and one that can be a very fine tightrope to walk. I've never been a wife or a mother so I can't speak from experience, but I don't think either you or Claire were in the wrong. She always intended to come back, and you never intended to push her away. If art carried a risk of serious injury would I still do it? I think I would as it's part of me, of my self-identity and the way I express myself."

Josh tried to scrub at his face, lifting his arm which had wrapped itself around Meg as she spoke. Her soothing words and gentle touch were a balm to his soul, but his body had held the strain of his grief and anger for too long and it all flowed out of him now. "I'm sorry," he whispered, embarrassed.

"Don't be, please," Meg shifted so that he could snuggle his face into the nook between her neck and shoulder, wrapping both arms around him, "I've got you, I've got you, let it all go."

Josh's body shook with the force of his outpouring and Meg did her best to shelter him through the storm, whispering words of compassion and reassurance. Not once did she tell him to calm down or that it was enough now, instead wanting him to get it all out. She wiped his tears with her thumb, stroked his hair back, and shed a few tears herself for the beautiful man who lay broken beside her and for the woman who had lost her life pursuing her own dreams.

THIRTEEN

"Why is the toilet and sink bright blue and the walls purple?" Betsie asked a couple of hours later as she returned from the bathroom and climbed up to snuggle between them in the bed, "And why does Daddy have no blankets? Did you not want to share, Meg? Aunt Jenna says at Little Acorns that we all have to share."

"Um," judging by the way she grabbed for the painkillers and gulped them down, Meg's head clearly hurt and Josh himself was not faring any better. They had managed to doze off a little before his daughter had come bouncing in, bright eyed and raring to start the day. Thank goodness it was Saturday and none of them had anywhere they needed to be. Snuggling like this though, all three of them together, was too much like a taste of what he and Betsie had missed out on, and Josh didn't want to let his mind go there. He had had enough of a cathartic outpouring for one weekend. Best put the shutters back up and not dwell on what might have been with his late wife or what would likely never be with the lovely woman who had held him tightly as his tears soaked through her pyjamas. Besides, the last thing he wanted was to confuse Betsie – he was already annoyed with himself for not being back in the lounge when she awoke.

"Come on little kangaroo, let's get you some breakfast at the café with Nana. You can show her you're feeling much better."

"You don't have to leave," Meg's eyes pleaded with him to stay but Josh knew she needed more rest.

"It's okay, I'll check on you later. In the meantime, phone me straight away if you feel worse or start going downhill at all. Please, promise me you will," he knew he sounded needy, but Josh didn't care. Meg had given him something so precious last night when she had listened and not judged, understood and held him, that he needed to know she was okay too.

"I will, but ah, you will come back soon, won't you?" Josh had to admit to being happy to hear his own desperation being echoed back to him, and came around to Meg's side of the bed. Betsie had bounced out to say goodbye to Bonnie and it was just the two of them for an all-too-brief moment.

He took Meg's hands in his as he perched on the edge of the mattress, "I will definitely see you this afternoon. I think I've used up all my babysitting credits though, so if you're feeling better, why don't the three of us go for a walk down by the harbour? We could get some fish and chips."

"That sounds lovely," Meg replied as he bent to kiss her gently on the forehead, deliberately avoiding her bruised bump, "thank you."

"No, thank you," Josh said, and they both knew what he was referring to.

Janet was surprised to see her son and granddaughter so early, appearing just as she was opening up for the day. She was even more surprised to see them both emerging from the new art shop across the road, but she said nothing about that and enveloped Betsie in a huge bear hug. Jenna had texted last night to ask her advice when the little one had seemed unwell, and when none of her suggestions for settling her granddaughter had worked, Janet had reluctantly advised that Jenna contact her brother. Ideally, Janet would've had her son be left in peace with the lovely Meg for the whole evening, hoping that the younger woman could chip away at the distant, often cold man that Josh had become since his tragic loss. As it was, it seemed that both man and girl had stayed the night with Meg and Janet couldn't hide her happiness for long.

"Morning! All okay? Meg doing well after the accident? My gorgeous granddaughter feeling better?" She gushed as they took the table nearest the counter. Janet hadn't even had a chance to turn on the stove or the kettle yet.

"Um, I think she got hot from crying so much, not a real high temperature at all," Josh said gruffly, though the smile he shot his daughter was full of indulgent affection.

"Ah well, I've told you before you need to leave her more often. So she gets used to it. You'd like a sleepover with Nanny wouldn't you, cherub?"

"Would there be sweeties?" Betsie was taking the offer very seriously, clearly settling in for hard negotiation and Josh shot his mother a look.

"Bear with a sore thumb again? Didn't get much sleep?" Janet whispered in his direction, forcing herself to refrain from following the question with a wink.

Betsie had the hearing of an eagle, however, and pounced on the reference, "No, Daddy didn't hit his thumb, silly, it was Meg who got hitted, on her head!" The girl giggled at her grandmother's apparent slow wittedness.

Josh rolled his eyes, in the direction which his daughter couldn't see, and Janet patted her little hand, "I know, love, I know."

"And is Meg okay?" Janet asked, seizing on the topic again, "You and she... doing okay?"

"Leave it off, Ma!" Josh snapped, feeling his face heating as memories of the previous twenty-four hours flooded in.

Janet nodded and busied herself getting breakfast for all three of them. He may be resisting it, but she'd seen the way those two looked at each other while they all waited for the ambulance to arrive yesterday. And if that was going to turn out to be purely platonic she'd eat her apron!

Despite the summer sun, the wind was bracing as the two adults walked down Oak Tree Lane, swinging the little girl between them. The street of shops curved at the sea end and became a cobbled pedestrian-only route which led directly down to the pier and the small harbour. In olden times this small inlet was known as Cheedlemouth, with the bay still being officially titled Cheedle Bay, being where the river Cheedle joined the North Sea. None of the locals called it by its map name, however, referring to it simply as Oak Bay.

Spotting Brin standing outside the fish and chip shop, and knowing that he often gave her an ice lolly from the small freezer inside, Betsie soon let go of them to run ahead.

"Be careful not to trip," Josh called to her as he and Meg watched his daughter's sandals flapping across the uneven stones.

Meg smiled up at him, feeling much better than she had earlier in the day. A long soak in a bubble bath, a good moisturise for her dehydrated skin and some scrambled eggs on toast and she felt like a new woman. The lump on her head remained, but now only pained her when it was touched.

"Feeling better?" Josh asked, studying her for any clue that she was masking her pain.

"Much," she replied, linking arms with him.

They hurried to catch up with Betsie, who had already been furnished with a push-up ice lolly despite not having eaten anything savoury yet. Meg was relieved that Josh didn't seem to mind, and hoped that this easy-going version of him might stay around a bit longer now that he'd got a lot off his chest. Whether they were to remain as friends or develop into something more, Meg was grateful for the intimate moments they had shared the previous day and night. She certainly wasn't going to push anything, however.

She had her own dreams to chase, and if Josh was adamant that that was a bad thing, then there would be no real future for them anyway.

FOURTEEN

The next week passed in a blur of sawing, sanding and hammering as the shop began to take shape. Both busy and clearly unsure as to where things stood with each other – or even where they wanted them to stand – Meg and Josh spent the hours treading a silent dance around each other which involved much 'accidental' brushing of skin, deep looks when they thought the other wasn't aware and the occasional high five when something turned out exactly as they'd both envisioned.

A comfortable working relationship, Meg would've described it as if asked – which Janet did. Often.

"I'll get her to back off," Josh said that Friday morning when his mother left having hand delivered some bacon butties and steaming coffees in takeaway Styrofoam cups.

"No need, she just wants to see you happy," Meg replied, studying his face for some indication as to how he felt. Josh had been a closed book since the previous weekend, and at times Meg struggled to believe they had shared such private details of themselves at all.

"Hmm," it came out almost as a growl and Meg raised her eyebrows, "sorry, sorry, just been a long week."

"It has," Meg agreed, though in truth she had enjoyed their time together and was reluctant to face the fact that today was the last day that Josh would be here working alongside her. To be fair, he'd had everything finished by yesterday afternoon, and seemed to be seeking out jobs to keep him here now – something which pleased Meg more than she'd like to admit. An extra layer of varnish here, a new hinge for that old cabinet over there…

Today it had no choice but to end, though, as Meg's best friend Lydia was arriving for a 'painting party' to get the shop ship shape for the grand opening. The celebration had been brought forward to the following weekend as Meg was keen for the place to start earning as soon as possible. At the moment, the cash was only flowing one way, and she feared the trickle was about to dry up altogether.

A loud honking from the road outside caught both their attention, and Meg knew without looking who it would be. Lydia never did anything quietly. Always had to make a grand entrance. But why she was five hours early, Meg had no idea. The opposite was normally the case, with the record being at one hour thirty-five minutes, when Meg had waited alone in a wine bar on the Quayside in Newcastle. Even then, Lydia had phoned to say they might as well just meet at the restaurant they'd booked, else they'd lose their reservation, the time for pre-dinner drinks having passed. Meg never chided nor complained, however, and often wondered if she needed more of those boundaries she was always reading about in self-help books.

"Um, I've started this final coat of varnish for the shelves here so I should probably keep going till it's finished," Josh said as Meg rushed to the window, desperately trying to shove her hair back up under her scarf. Lydia was never anything but pristine, and Meg had hoped she'd at least have time for a shower before her friend arrived. Sensing excitement, Bonnie stretched languidly and ventured out of the basket that was kept at the bottom of the staircase at the back of the shop, deliberately placed so that she wouldn't get mixed up in any of the DIY.

"You look gorgeous just as you are," Josh walked over and stilled her hands in his own, as Meg realised she had been muttering to herself about what a state she must look.

It was the first overtly deliberate physical contact he had made with her all week, and the timing couldn't have been worse. Meg was reluctant to pull away as the hairs on her arms stood up from the almost electrical connection between them and a tingling heat followed in their wake. Nevertheless, Lydia was no doubt already attracting attention on Oak Tree Lane, with her vibrant red hair and skin-tight outfit.

Catching a glimpse through the window, Josh gave a small whistle, "WowWee, she'll have old Derek across the road in a dead faint on his butcher's block if he catches sight of her. Bit of a ladies' man," Josh winked, but Meg pulled her hands away. It was the same effect Lydia had on men everywhere and Meg had long since gotten used to it. Admittedly, through gritted teeth at times when her friend made a play for someone she knew Meg had been interested in first.

Anyway, that was all water under the bridge. Lydia

had been right about Chris and wouldn't be in the village long enough to go on her usual manhunt. Certainly, there was no local nightlife to speak of, unless you counted the tavern which wasn't exactly overflowing with eligible bachelors.

"I really should get going," Josh said awkwardly as Lydia tried to press a glass of prosecco into his hands. He had politely rebuffed her efforts at flirting for the past hour and now made a deliberate show of turning his back to her. *What kind of friend would ignore the person they'd come to see and try to hit it off with their hired help instead?* He'd been patient for Meg's sake, but enough was enough. He would just finish up washing his brushes in the sink here then he'd be off. Shame there wasn't any water downstairs or he wouldn't have chanced coming into the flat at all. Apparently Lydia disliked animals, so Bonnie was taking shelter with him in the bathroom, with Josh now wishing he'd locked them in to keep a certain person out.

Meg had looked embarrassed, then annoyed and now had a blank smile of resignation as she was joined again on the sofa by her guest. Josh had never seen this side of her, the one who hid her genuine feelings behind a mask of servility and civility. He imagined this was the little Meg of whom she had spoken last weekend – people pleasing and passively accepting of whatever was doled out to her. It made Josh angry and he slowed his task so that he could hear what the women were talking about. He shouldn't have been eavesdropping, he knew, but they were aware he was still there, and that the door between them was open, so he figured they'd save anything private to say later.

"So, you got here quick," Meg said, placing her mug of prosecco on the floor. She only had two wine glasses, and Lydia had insisted one be for Josh, despite him declining more than once. It was far too early in her busy day for bubbly stuff, but as per usual Meg had been outvoted by her overbearing friend.

"Ah, yes well about that Meggy, I'm afraid I have to be getting off again in an hour or two, so just the one bottle of prosecco between us, eh?"

"I would say just the one glass," Meg was horrified that her friend would be so blasé about driving after consuming so much alcohol and so made a point of putting the bottle on the floor at her side of the sofa. *Out of sight, out of mind,* she hoped.

Lydia's face betrayed her momentary anger at being denied, but she plastered her permanent fake smile back on and continued, "Yes, well, anyway I have a hot date tonight back in the city so our little painting party will have to be postponed."

"But I thought you were staying the weekend? If you aren't here to help then why didn't you just call?" Meg asked, confused. Lydia rarely did anything that wasn't wholeheartedly convenient for herself. Something Meg had only wised up to in the past six months or so when no help with packing or moving had been forthcoming. Meg had never made friends easily and had often realised well into each relationship that she tended to attract 'takers' when she herself was very much a 'giver'. So, in the end she had been left with just Chris and Lydia, everyone else having disappeared over the years when she tried to speak up for herself.

"What? Oh, I just offered to do that after my breakup with Tony the other week, when I thought a little jaunt in the countryside with a hot farmer might perk me up. I'm with Ciaran now so obviously I'll be spending time with him. Honeymoon phase, you know how it is."

Meg really didn't, but she said nothing about that. She'd only ever been with Chris and the early days of their relationship could hardly be considered 'heady.'

She waited for Lydia to continue as there was obviously something she'd come to say.

"So, ah, I thought we could have a little tête-à-tête," Lydia went on, moving closer to Meg in a conspiratorial manner, "about Christopher."

"I broke up with Chris when I moved here, there's nothing more to say about him, is there? I mean, he was never your favourite person, not since he chose me and not you when we first met him and his mate on that night out in Durham."

"Well, actually there is, darling, something more to say," Lydia twirled the stem of her glass around between her fingers, a smug smile on her lips, "I was at the Raven's Club with Ciaran last Saturday night – you know the exclusive members' one off the golf course – and I happened to see Chris have an almighty row with a rather leggy blonde. Great entertainment it was. From what I and everyone else could hear, she was dumping him because he wasn't giving her any more attention than he had when you and he were still living together."

"What?" Meg asked, blindsided.

"Cheating, for months it would seem, if not years. Just as I'd suspected," Lydia tapped her glass with an inch long acrylic fingernail and looked very pleased with herself.

"So, just to clarify, you drove for over an hour to tell me 'I told you so,'" Meg could feel her voice rising in pitch and Bonnie hopped up onto her lap, no doubt keen to reassure herself that nothing was wrong. Meg was suddenly aware of the tap still running in the bathroom, of the heat in the stuffy room that had only one painted-shut window on the back wall, and the faintly foisty smell that was an ever-present gift from the old carpet.

"Now, now Meggy, no need to get your knickers in a twist. I told you that you were well rid of him…"

Lydia didn't have a chance to expound on her point as Meg jumped up suddenly, knocking her mug over in the process. She watched as the bubbly liquid was quickly sucked into the shaggy, brown carpet, leaving no mark in its wake. Her hands were shaking, her whole body shaking in fact, and the kitten beside her was howling in indignation at having been so unjustly toppled from her knee.

"I think you should leave," the gravelly voice from behind them caused both women to turn suddenly. To be honest, Meg had forgotten Josh was still there.

"I beg your pardon!" Lydia was on her feet as well now.

"You've said what you came to say, I think it's time to go, if Meg agrees?" He looked reassuringly in her direction and Meg was suddenly overcome with emotion.

Rage, relief, shame, she couldn't hold them back.

"Yes, please go Lydia. I've started a new life here. A fresh slate. And I'm slowly realising that I don't want to be the old Meg any longer. Thanks for coming. Bye." A loud sob followed as Meg ran to her bedroom. It felt like a very teenagery thing to do, but she couldn't bear for either her former best friend or Josh to see the ugly crying that she was about to do.

FIFTEEN

Meg heard the two sets of steps tramping down the old stairs, the now-familiar squeak on the three closest to the bottom, as she curled on her side on top of her bed in the foetal position. A small mewling heralded the arrival of Bonnie, who was too small to get up onto the mattress unaided. Tears streaming down her face unheeded, and her nose swiftly following suit, Meg bent down and brought the little kitten up to her, leaving a damp patch on the cat's head where she snuggled her face into the soft fur before letting Bonnie curl up in the curve of her body.

"Well, that's that, Bonnie," Meg spoke haltingly when she could catch enough breath between her tears, "that was my last person, last friend and now she's gone. I know, I know, it was a toxic friendship which I should've distanced myself from years ago, but the truth is without Aunt Connie, without Chris and now Lydia I have no one." The sobs wracked her body and Meg gave into them.

"You have me, and Betsie and my mam and Jenna, and most of the village I should suspect. You saw how many people came to check on you while we waited for the ambulance last week. Apart from Mrs. Jasper from number twenty. She sees anything gossip worthy as a spectator sport!" Josh tried to bring some levity to the situation.

Startled by the voice of the man behind her, Meg simply replied, "I thought you'd left. Do you not need to collect Betsie?"

"Jenna is keeping her a while longer. I've got time. May I join you?"

"Huh?"

"On the bed. Can I lay down with you for a bit?"

Meg didn't have the headspace to think about it. Her mind was clouded with sadness and embarrassment, yet she didn't want to be alone, "Alright then."

She remained where she was, facing the window that looked out onto Oak Tree Lane below. Realising randomly that she needed a new blind. She felt the dip of the mattress as he carefully lowered his body behind her, the warmth as he shuffled close and became the big spoon to her small one.

"I'm sorry," Josh whispered into her hair.

He was close enough for the tingles to begin in her body from his nearness, yet Meg was sure not a single part of them below the neck was actually touching the other. *Ever the gentleman,* she thought as she replied, "Why are you sorry? You didn't cheat on me. You didn't come here to gloat."

"I'm sorry that they didn't value you. That they hurt you, when I reckon you're the least deserving of anyone's bad treatment. It seems to me that you always see the best in people, always try to help others, and they abused that. You're well rid of them, Meg, but you're certainly not alone. I promise."

His words had the tears ramping up again, until Meg's body was once more wracked with sobs.

"Aw, seeing you like this is breaking my heart, honey, can I hold you?"

Meg gave a muffled yes without allowing herself to overthink it. Immediately, Josh's strong arm reached over her, pulling her flush against his body. Meg's back pressed against his hard torso and instinctively she tangled her feet with his.

"I'm a fool," she whispered, clinging onto his arm around her waist like a lifeline, "and now I'm a lonely fool. To be honest, I've been lonely since Aunt Connie died. It was only my dreams that kept me warm in the dark hours when the grief of her passing took hold. The dreams for this place that she and I had shared."

"I understand, and look at you, making them a reality, she would be so proud," Meg could feel his words whispered against the shell of her ear, "and I know loneliness, really I do, I could do with some help in that department myself." His hand took hers where it rested on top of the blanket and they both lay there in silence for a moment, each lost in their own thoughts and memories.

At length, Meg rolled over to face him, trailing a finger down Josh's face from his temple to his chin. He leant into her touch and she felt his body relax as she cupped his cheek.

"You're so beautiful," he whispered, lifting a shaking hand and hovering it beside her face as if she was too delicate to touch.

"With my runny nose and swollen, red eyes? I doubt it! I'm not a pretty crier," Meg replied, though inside she revelled at the idea he found her beautiful. To prove her point, though, she wiped her nose on her sleeve indecorously.

Bonnie chose this moment to use the couple as a climbing frame, leaving her spot on the other side of Meg and clawing her way up Meg's back before jumping to Josh's shoulder and using his back as a slide. She made herself comfortable on the spare pillow behind him, as if she had every right to do so and Meg couldn't help but smile.

"Ouch! Her little claws are sharp," Josh said, the spell between them broken for a moment.

"Big baby!" Meg teased, poking him gently in the chest.

They both laughed, until the playful moment once again became something more and Josh became very still, looking into Meg's eyes intently. She could feel his heavy breaths, understood their meaning and without any consideration for her still-damp face, Meg slowly lowered her lips to his, keeping eye contact until the very last moment.

Softly at first, and then with an increasing urgency which bordered on desperation, they poured all of their past hurts and all of their future hopes into that shared connection. It was a kiss, nothing more and nothing less, but Meg felt it right down to her toes. It was the most sensual sensation she had ever had from physical contact and the physicality of it made her lightheaded.

"Was that okay? I'd never want you to think I was taking advantage," Josh asked when they came up for air, the worry lines back on his forehead as he watched carefully for any sign of regret in her expression.

"I started it," Meg smiled and was rewarded with a big grin. He stroked her back with his fingertips, up and down, up and down in a rhythm that might well have sent Meg to sleep – emotionally spent as she was with her crying from earlier – yet she knew nothing could keep her from wanting to experience that kiss again. To make sure the feelings were not a fluke. A 'first time lucky' kind of thing.

No better time than the present, she told herself, wondering fleetingly where this new-found confidence had come from and how long it would stay.

Josh wanted nothing more than to curl up with Meg as the sun set and night cocooned them in their little nest. As it was, it was the middle of summer, the sun wouldn't set for at least another four hours and he had a little girl to feed and bathe. As delicious as the kisses were, as relaxed and at home he felt, another part of his heart was still playing dollies with her aunt Jenna, probably asking where he was, and so Josh was getting antsy. Torn. That was it. He felt torn he realised, and guilty too for putting his desires first for once, and it wasn't a nice feeling at all.

"You should go and collect her, get back home in time for your nighttime routine," Meg said, as if reading his mind.

"I'm sorry, it's just…"

"Don't ever apologise for having Betsie. Please. She's your priority and that's exactly as it should be," Meg smiled, meaning every word. She reached out to soothe his worry lines and Josh leaned into her touch.

"Thank you," he whispered, "for being you. For understanding."

"Always," Meg replied, enjoying the kisses which he dotted around her face and her neck, like little butterflies caressing her skin finally landing on the tip of her nose. When he paused for a moment to catch her eye, his own gaze smouldering with the promise of things yet to come between them, Meg took the opportunity to capture his lips with her own one last time. Playfully, she teased him with her mouth until neither could play the slow dance any longer, and the tempo sped up to match their heartbeats.

SIXTEEN

Meg had been painting all morning. The job that she had planned to share with Lydia now felt pretty daunting by herself. But she was tackling it one wall at a time, grateful that Josh had helped her lift the old lino earlier in the week and that the new flooring wouldn't be delivered till Tuesday. This meant that she could be more haphazard with paint splatters, something her old dungarees could attest to.

Wiping a splash of paint from her nose, Meg was surprised to see the outline of two familiar figures through the glass panel of the front door. She and Josh hadn't made any plans before he left yesterday and she hadn't made any assumptions that she would see him this weekend, yet here he was with a very excited little girl who had even brought her own paintbrush.

"Meg! Daddy says you need help and that we're the people to do it!"

"Does he now?" Meg smiled up at Josh as Betsie pushed past her into the small shop space.

"Yes, like Bob the Builder!"

Meg didn't get the reference, but it was immaterial as the butterflies in her stomach had started the moment she saw the man who had been in her dreams all night. As if an unspoken agreement passed between the two adults, neither showed any affection to the other that might make the sharp little girl think they were anything more than friends. They laughed through their jobs, though, the three of them, as Josh made quick work of the walls and the two girls focused on what would be the children's corner.

"I think we should call it Silly Splats," Betsie declared, admiring her handiwork on the wall, where a distinct oak tree made from fingerprints was surrounded by splashes and blotches of paint in all colours and shapes.

"It's a deal," Meg said happily, setting down her own

brush and straightening her protesting back, "do you think your friends will want to visit the Silly Splats corner?"

"Umm," Betsie said, a look of serious concentration on her face, "will there be biscuits?"

"Yes, and juice, once everyone is finished their painting."

"It's a deal!" Betsie parroted her words back to her and Meg staggered backwards as she was jumped on for a full hug from the infant.

She caught Josh's eye over Betsie's mop of curls and couldn't tear her gaze away from the warmth she saw there.

As if he was quite overcome from the scene before him, Josh laid his brush on the paint pot lid and declared, "We deserve cake. I'll pop across to Mam's."

And with that he was gone, leaving Meg feeling slightly bereft even though she knew he'd be back in a matter of minutes.

"I don't have a mummy," Betsie said thoughtfully when the hug ended and Meg was gathering the smaller paintbrushes she and Betsie had used.

Meg paused in her task, aware this was a sensitive subject and she must tread carefully, "Neither do I. My mummy went to heaven when I was born."

"My mummy is in heaven too, with your mummy," Betsie said, clapping her hands as if that was extremely good news.

"My daddy is there too," Meg added, hoping to further their growing bond even more.

Her words didn't have the desired effect, however, quite the opposite in fact, as Meg watched Betsie's little face crumple.

"Daddies can't go to heaven!" The little girl wailed, sinking to the floor with her head down, "I don't want my daddy to go to heaven with yours. He's mine. He needs to stay here."

Meg dropped to the floor, ignoring the open tins of paint and wet splatters, gathering the girl into her arms, rubbing her heaving little back and rocking her gently in her lap. She didn't have a chance to even begin to explain, however, as at that moment Josh walked back in, a paper plate full of Victoria sponge balancing on two cups of coffee, and a juice box almost squashed under his arm.

"What's happened? Did she hurt herself?" His words were barely audible over his daughter's sobs and Josh dumped everything on the nearest surface to scoop her out of Meg's arms.

"No, we were just…" Meg began but she was quickly interrupted.

"I don't want you to go to heaven, Daddy! Please stay!"

"What's this, honey? I'm not going anywhere," he stroked Betsie's hair where she clung to his neck and shot a wide eyed look to Meg who hovered beside the pair uncomfortably now, feeling absolutely awful. She was clearly not cut out to be mother material.

"I'm sorry, I'm so sorry, I shouldn't be trusted with…" the remainder of the sentence was muffled as she turned her back to hide her own tears. She clasped her hands and began wringing them together – a sign of her anxiety which had survived since childhood. She knew Josh would be angry, had every right to be angry. After all, she had just confused his child to an extent that only a lot of patient explanation had any chance of settling the girl.

Even then, what permanent damage might she have done?

The guilt rose, thick and fast up Meg's throat and she ran upstairs to throw it up.

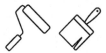

Josh knew Meg would never do or say anything to deliberately upset Betsie and so followed her upstairs, his daughter in his arms, her wet face snuggled into the crook of his neck.

"I'm right here. Not going anywhere. Nothing to worry about," he whispered as he took the stairs two at a time, careful to step over the little kitten who was snoozing on the top landing as if she didn't have a worry in the world.

Josh sat on the sofa with Betsie curled up on his lap, the two of them chatting quietly about what had happened, until the sound of the toilet flushing indicated Meg was finished.

"Oh! I didn't think you'd come up, I mean I thought you'd want to get as far away from me as possible," Meg blurted, "I know I certainly do, if that were at all within the realms of… I mean, ah…"

"Come here, honey," he said softly, lying his spare arm along the back of the sofa beside him in invitation, "come here and have a cuddle with me and Betsie."

Meg struggled to hide her shock. Not that she didn't know Josh to be compassionate and supportive, but rather that she didn't feel like she deserved forgiveness. Nevertheless, her feet made the choice for her as she slipped into the space next to them, letting Josh move her against his side with his arm around her shoulder.

"Betsie has told me why she got upset, and I've explained that people normally only go to heaven when they are old or very ill. We've talked about how Nanny and Brin are still alive and they're older than me, even Mrs. Jasper is still going strong with her walking frame and she must be positively ancient."

"She doesn't like people touching it," Betsie nodded, as if this were a very important piece of information, "especially children."

Meg nodded along, whilst her mind was simultaneously whirring with the idea that something so big could be sorted so calmly and rationally. Having grown up with her father's outbursts, and having spent the first decade of her life walking on eggshells, Meg found this a hard concept to grasp.

"So Daddy is staying, and so are you," Betsie declared,

as if voicing the fact was all it took to have it be the truth, grabbing Meg's hand in her own much smaller one.

"Yes, definitely, I mean, I'm sorry I confused…"

"Shhh," Josh murmured against her hair, "Betsie knows, I know, there's nothing to apologise for."

And they sat there, the three of them, snuggling closely, grateful that they were indeed all still here.

SEVENTEEN

Tomorrow was the big day. The grand opening. The culmination of years of dreaming and planning. Meg was partly exhausted, partly unable to rest due to the nervous energy which coursed through her body. Other than a few waves through the shop window and bumping into each other in the tearoom as they both grabbed a quick takeaway, she and Josh hadn't seen each other that week. Tonight though, tonight he was taking her out on their first official date. It was only to the tavern by The Tree, but the location mattered not a jot to Meg, so desperate was she to see the man and to spend quality time with him.

The term 'date' in itself caused Meg to have more than

a flutter of nerves, and she had spent a long time choosing her outfit and curling her hair for the occasion. She couldn't recall Josh ever seeing her with make-up on, so she hoped he would be impressed at how well she scrubbed up. Better than the paint-splattered, wild-haired version at least.

Meg arrived early so that she could talk to the landlord, Matty, about making her use of the back room for art classes a more permanent thing. Her first two taster sessions had been a success – well, there had only been four attendees at the first and six at the second, despite offering them with fifty percent off what would be the normal price, but Meg was hopeful that numbers would increase as word got out. She loved the way her little studio gallery had turned out, but on reflection it was nowhere near big enough to accommodate more than one-to-one adult tuition, and small children's groups. So, she had decided to forge ahead with providing those from her shop, as well as selling art supplies and paintings of course, and hoped to make a mutually beneficial alliance with the tavern for the bigger classes.

Matty seemed delighted with the idea, and Robyn too, giving Meg the distinct impression everyone in the area was keen to diversify their income sources as much as possible. Which was only sensible, she knew, given their very rural location and lack of footfall. Josh arrived as they were finalising details, and other than a quick hello he disappeared straight off to the table in the farthest corner. There was no live music this evening, so they had the whole place to choose from with just a few dedicated locals sitting bored at the bar.

"What can I get you to drink?" Meg asked, approaching Josh who had his head buried in an official looking document.

"Pardon? Oh sorry, I drove here so just half a lager shandy please. Get yourself a proper drink, though, I can drop you back on the way to collect Betsie from my mam's."

His tone was a bit off and Meg's stomach sank. He had barely looked up, never mind made note of her appearance. She felt a lot less confident when she joined him, drinks in hand and a menu for the limited bar food under her arm.

"Is everything okay?" Meg asked hesitantly as she took the seat opposite him.

"Yep, all fine," Josh said, as if on automatic pilot, before looking up, sighing, and clearly deciding he owed her more honesty than that, "actually, not really."

"Would you like to talk about it?"

"I'm not making this much of a first date am I?" He leant forward and pecked her on the lips. "Sorry, I meant to buy flowers from that fancy place down the road from me, but I got a letter from the bank then had a protracted call with my accountant and another with my solicitor, all with Betsie bouncing round in the background, so I haven't had much headspace for romance. Sorry."

"Please don't keep apologising," Meg reached over and stroked his hand which still held the letter. She noticed it was trembling slightly and continued," I'd rather you were open with me. Goodness knows, I've piled enough of my own baggage onto you in the past few weeks."

Josh placed the letter down on the table and laced his fingers between hers, "The building I live in was passed down in Claire's family and she received her inheritance just after we married when her grandad died. The building, that is, there was no cash involved, that all went to her parents as her father was an only child. So, we were asset rich and cash poor, especially since the art gallery was passed to Claire, her brother, and her father equally. Neither of the men had any desire to run the place, so a legally binding agreement was made, whereby her brother relinquished his interest in return for his third of the monetary value, and her father agreed to take a share of the profits but to have no responsibility for upkeep or anything like that, until the time – if it ever came – when Claire wished to move on, in which case he would be due a third of the proceeds of the sale."

"That all sounds very complicated," Meg said.

"It is, especially since neither of us had life insurance when Claire died. Stupid, I know, but we were young and foolish. She had travel insurance, though the cover was restricted since it was an extreme sport she was participating in. So, her parents paid for the repatriation of her body, I paid for the funeral, and I was left with my home, the art shop below and the contract they had all previously signed."

"Do her parents live nearby?" Meg asked gently, thinking that was a heavy burden for a grieving husband and father to bear.

"No, Somerset, so Betsie and I rarely see them. Claire had taken a mortgage out on the building to pay her share of her brother's third when they initially received the inheritance, plus a small business loan to get the place updated, decorated and so on. She never really got round to that, what with pregnancy, her climbing and everything. Then she died, and I used what was left of the loan for Betsie and me to live on. I know it wasn't wise, but I was drowning in grief and had very little income from the gallery which remained closed for many months. Couldn't bear to set foot in there for ages, to be honest. Anyway, now it's apparently crunch time. I'm behind with the repayments on both the mortgage and the loan, the obvious answer is to sell up, pay Claire's dad his share and draw a line under it…" he scrubbed a hand across his face and took a large gulp of his drink, the menu forgotten on the table beside them.

"But emotionally that feels very final, and maybe a bit of a betrayal?" Meg hedged.

"Exactly," Josh's face relaxed and she saw the first hint of a smile since he'd arrived, "I should've known you'd understand."

"I do, and I think the emotions surrounding it all are very complex and no one can make the decision but you. That said, I'm not sure how you can go on trying to keep the business afloat when your heart's not in it. You want to be carving and designing not selling pictures or liaising with artists and there's nothing wrong with that. You're allowed to have your own passions, Josh, and to forego other things in order to pursue them. The fact that you're such a talented carpenter and can make a living from what fires your interest is a huge bonus. Not everyone is that lucky."

"I know, I know, I don't have long to decide now, the clock's ticking. Then there's the problem that it's not just a business, it's our home above it. The only home Betsie's ever known. I could move us in with Jenna, I suppose, now that Mam's moved above the tearoom…" he stared off into the distance, caught up in his thoughts.

"I tell you what," Meg said, downing what was left of her spiced rum and coke, "why don't we ditch the meal out plan and go for a wander by The Tree to clear your head. Then you could come back to mine and I'll make us something to eat, how does that sound?"

"Like I'm a very lucky man who needs to buck his ideas up," Josh's expression was pure gratitude with a smidgen of rueful awareness and Meg couldn't help but lean forward and peck him on the cheek.

"Come on then, I'll give you a chance to do better," she winked as he gathered up the worrisome letter and shoved it back in his pocket.

EIGHTEEN

Josh had lived in the Oakley area all his life and never once had he made a wish at the old oak. Meg, however, seemed to think the whole experience completely normal, placing her palms flat against the wide trunk, squeezing her eyes tight shut and asking for something that only she was privy to. Josh, on the other hand, felt extremely silly despite there being no one to see them.

Nevertheless, what harm could it do? He asked himself as he followed Meg's example and made his own silent plea.

"No prizes for guessing what my wish was, but what was yours, I wonder?" Josh mused as they headed back to his van hand in hand.

"Ah, now that's a secret. Maybe I'll share if it comes true," Meg smiled up at him, keen now to get back to her place and have the man to herself.

Josh hadn't planned for the evening to end up back at Meg's flat. He had to collect Betsie by eleven, so had a good few hours yet, but he had hoped to wine and dine Meg properly, the way she deserved. Not for the first time that evening he admired how gorgeous she looked, wondering as they drove the short distance back to Oak Tree Lane if he'd actually voiced that thought.

"You look beautiful by the way," he felt himself blushing at the admission.

"Oh! Thank you," Meg's cheeks began to heat too, but he could tell in his brief sideways glances that she was pleased with the compliment. The feeling of her hand resting just above his knee as he drove, the sun low in the sky and the promise of the evening ahead relaxed his fraught nerves, so that by the time they arrived back at Brush Stroaks his shoulders held none of the tension Josh had felt in the pub.

The energy of mutual awareness crackled between the pair as they made their way up the stairs and into

Meg's flat. As soon as they reached the living room,
Meg stopped abruptly catching Josh off guard.
Following behind her, he had been focused on the
bounce in her curls, imagining wrapping one dark lock
around his finger and watching as it sprang free. He
couldn't hide his surprise therefore, when Meg was
suddenly facing him, her expression part questioning,
part demanding as she locked eyes with him, her arms
coming up around Josh's neck in the same moment,
and her face angled to the right as she closed the gap
between them.

He may have been surprised, but he certainly wasn't
disappointed, and Josh welcomed her searching lips
eagerly, feeling passion flare between them from the
first touch. There was no tentative teasing this time, no
apprehensive appraisal of the other's willingness to
proceed. Instead, the electricity that arced between
their joined mouths was positively combustible.
Without being aware of it, Josh moved them both so
that Meg was against the wall, and now she pulled him
so close that her body was almost melting into his. No
space between them to determine where one ended
and the other began. Josh had one hand in her
beautiful curls, the other stroking down her side, over
her ribs to rest gently on her hip.

They paused for breath, Meg's hands still tangled in

his hair, her eyes hooded and love-drunk, a perfect reflection of his own he was sure. She let go a small sigh of contentment, and he cupped her cheek with the hand that had been playing with her curls.

"You're so beautiful," Josh repeated his words from earlier, though this time Meg's cheeks were already flushed from the passionate embrace they'd shared.

"So are you," she replied, her eyes searching his, "perhaps now would be the time to see more of each other?" Her whispered question caught him off guard. Not because his mind wasn't already going there, but because of the shy way she'd said it. That in itself was such a perfect invitation, such a turn on.

His own reply, which Josh had intended to whisper into the shell of Meg's ear, was however drowned out by a heavy banging on the door below. He sprang away, his heart thumping wildly in his chest, his first thought being of his daughter before he remembered his mother would phone if there was a problem. She had no idea that he was just across the road at Meg's flat, after all. Nevertheless, a huge ball of guilt lodged itself in Josh's stomach as he sought the source of the intrusive noise.

Meg blinked twice in quick succession, trying to bring her mind back from the deliciously heady place it had been in Josh's arms. She felt suddenly cold as the warmth of his body disappeared, his footsteps on the stairs being the thing which finally snapped her out of their loved-up cocoon.

"Who are you? Where's Meg?" the barked questions, delivered in a condescending and haughty tone which she would recognise anywhere, had Meg hurrying down the stairs to interject herself between the two men. Her legs felt shaky – unfortunately no longer from Josh's sweet touch – and her breath came in short, anxious gasps.

"Chris, what are you doing here?

He ignored the question and attempted to push past her into the shop. Meg stood her ground, not wanting him in her new space – the one that had never been polluted by his negativity or criticisms. Meg heard Josh behind her breathing heavily. She felt the weight of his support, yet at the same time knew that she wanted to do this alone. To stand up to her ex-partner the way she should've done years ago.

"You moved on fast!" The angry man continued with his barrage of exclamations, thrusting an angry finger in Josh's direction as Meg turned calmly to speak to him.

"I can handle this. Really. You go back up, I'll be there in a minute," there was a newfound calmness in her voice that Meg felt proud of. Josh couldn't hide the reluctance in his eyes, but immediately submitted to her request.

"Just call if he gets …" he backed away slowly, his eyes filled with gentle sincerity never leaving hers, until just before he reached the counter at the back of the shop where Josh flicked his gaze upwards and shot her ex a warning glare.

"I will, I will," Meg turned her attention to Chris then, "you've got a cheek coming here, Chris. And to accuse me of moving on fast, well that's laughable isn't it!"

Chris had never seen this side of Meg. The one where she stood up for herself. The one where she called him out on his hypocrisy. Predictably, he tried to bluster his way out of it, "I don't know what's come over you, Meggy. Have you been drinking? Did that man spike your drink?"

"Don't be ridiculous, Chris, and certainly stop trying to

tar others with your own brush. I'm surprised Lydia hasn't already told you how she did her civic duty and informed me of your wayward ways."

"Meggy, let me explain, she must be mistaken, I…" That whiny schoolboy voice full of obsequious denial was grating on her last nerve.

"There's really no need for explanations, Chris, none at all. I understand perfectly. You were cheating on me. Repeatedly. Walked all over me for most of our relationship. I can only thank my lucky stars now that I got this place in my own name. All mine. So if you don't mind, I was in the middle of a very pleasant evening." She indicated towards the street behind him.

"Please Meggy, I've changed my mind, we can live out our dream."

"My dream, Chris, it was always only ever mine and Aunt Connie's. I have the feeling you were only playing along the whole time. What were you after? My inheritance? Someone sensible to bring home to your parents so they wouldn't cut you off the way they'd threatened to?"

"Meggy, listen, I need…" he was positively begging now but Meg was having none of it. She'd evidently put her big girl pants on today and felt a confidence that had alluded her for all of her adult life up till now.

"What is it, Chris? Not that I have any care what you need, but… Did you bed the wrong person? Have a go at the boss's wife and lose your job?"

The spluttered expletives and beads of sweat which stood out on his forehead told Meg that she had hit the nail on the head, and she silently admitted to feeling a small amount of pleasure at seeing her ex so uncomfortable.

"Sorry, Chris, this ship sailed a long time ago. You'll need to find another unsuspecting woman to leech off. Goodbye," and with that Meg shut the door, firmly and resolutely, on her old life.

She took a moment to take in the sight of him through the glass, his tie askew and his shirt untucked, before Chris turned away with a look of shock in his eyes.

How the worm has turned, Meg thought to herself, enjoying the deep sense of satisfaction from closing the door on her past as she went to rejoin her future.

NINETEEN

Josh had listened to the interaction, cheering Meg on silently from the stairwell and ready to welcome her into his arms once she'd seen Chris off with his tail between his legs.

"What's this?" He asked gently, pulling away from their embrace as soon as he heard the telltale sniffing, "Why the tears? You were magnificent down there, Meg."

"I don't know, relief I guess," she looked up at him with a watery smile, "pride in myself for once. I feel like I've turned a corner. Found my voice and my independence."

She pulled away then and went to put the kettle on, picking up a mewling Bonnie as she went and snuggling her close. Meg was well aware of the contradiction of what she'd just said, spoken as it was against Josh's chest.

She had found her independence and was about to give some of it away again. *Was that what she really wanted?* She turned to look at Josh who'd sat down on the sofa, himself deep in thought.

Was he thinking the same? Wondering if entwining their lives would be the right thing to do? He had a small child and so even more at stake than she did.

They drank their tea in companiable silence, the deep purrs of the kitten the noisiest thing in the room. It didn't feel awkward or uncomfortable, but Meg couldn't deny that the easiness of earlier had been replaced by the heaviness that they'd experienced back in the tavern. Clearly, they both had a lot on their minds and now wasn't the night to discuss it, not with the grand opening of her little art shop tomorrow and Josh being in limbo as to what to do with his own business holdings.

No, Meg decided to call it a night, citing the big day ahead as a reason for turning in early. Josh didn't disagree, seeming if anything rather too eager to get on his way and collect Betsie. The heated kisses from earlier were replaced with a quick peck goodbye and a promise to be there tomorrow for the celebration, before Josh disappeared quickly, leaving Meg feeling unsettled and needy. Clearly her body hadn't got the memo that she was a strong, independent woman now, and Meg wasn't sure a bubble bath was going to help alleviate that feeling.

A distinct lack of sleep made Meg's actions sluggish the next morning as she made the final preparations for Brush Stroaks' grand opening. Excitement and nerves for the day ahead were no doubt the cause of her sudden insomnia, along with a frustrating niggle, like an itch she couldn't scratch, that things had been left unresolved between herself and Josh the night before.

Popping into the Acorn and Squirrel tearoom to collect the cakes that she'd ordered for the opening, Meg was faced with a quizzical Janet, keen to know why her son had collected Betsie some two hours earlier than scheduled the night before.

"I, ah, believe he was distracted by some business

issues," Meg was deliberately vague.

"Yes, well the sooner he sorts those out the better for all concerned," Janet nodded sagely as she handed Meg the three cake boxes, one stacked precariously on top of the other, "I'm hoping he might get an offer today that even he can't refuse."

The cryptic comment was not lost on Meg though she simply thanked the woman and left, refusing to be lured into seeking any clarification. This was her day, the day her dreams of becoming an art shop owner in Oakley became true, and Meg was just selfish enough to want nothing to distract her from that. She couldn't help her mind chugging along on its own track, however, as she rearranged the cupcakes on their stands for the third time back in the studio.

Was Josh the right person at the wrong time? Not the right person at all, but simply a rebound attachment after her breakup? Or, conversely, the one she'd been meant to find all along?

Meg scraped her hands through her hair out of habit, then remembered she'd had her curls freshly washed and set the day before at the salon up in Upper Oakley. She had opted to not go the cheapest route for once and so had avoided the quaint hairdressers in Lower Oakley, which still retained the overhead hood hairdryers from the '50s. Having her curls tamed for once, Meg was trying hard not to touch them and reduce the whole style to frizz before her guests arrived.

Now lacking a preoccupation, she caught herself wringing her hands and forced them apart, swivelling on one foot to take in the whole of the little area. The children's corner was bright and welcoming with paints for fingerpainting, small brushes for tiny hands and two big beanbags for those who didn't want to be confined to the little table and chairs. There were two miniature easels and some simple 'how-to' books for those who could read.

The walls around the rest of the space were a warm cream, heavily laden with watercolour landscapes in oak frames, oil still-life paintings framed by a metallic gilt effect, and a few portraits outlined in jazzy colours. Meg had hoped to appeal to as wide a clientele as possible until she learnt what would sell and what wouldn't in her small corner of the world. Some of the art was her own work but the majority were pieces which she had been buying and stashing away for the past few years, in anticipation of this very moment.

As she restacked the flyers on the smooth counter top, which would give information on her classes and

prices, Meg looked at the clock on the back wall and
sighed heavily. Up early because she had been too
excited to sleep, there were still four hours until the
grand opening. Plenty of time – too much, in fact, to be
waiting idly and giving the nerves a chance to settle in
– so Meg decided to wrap her soft curls in a gentle
scarf and to have a wander down to the harbour. The
summer sun shone brightly with only a slight breeze,
so she hoped to not return too dishevelled from the
outing.

Of course, Meg hadn't banked on seeing the very man
that had left her tossing and turning into the wee
hours. If anything – or anyone – was certain to have
her heart pumping faster and her face blushing so hot
as to melt her carefully applied make-up, it was him.
Feeling the droplets of sweat accumulating under the
band of her headscarf and hoping the damp wouldn't
reach her curls, Meg decided the best course of action
by far would be to turn quietly and return the way she
had come as quickly as possible. Her feet had barely
touched the cobbles after all, so it would be quite
possible to discreetly…

"Meg! Daddy, look! It's Meg!"

Too late, she had already been spotted by the eagle eyes of the youngster, who was now barrelling towards her at a rate sure to end in skinned knees and screams. In order to avoid both, Meg hurried towards the girl, catching her in her arms and nearly being knocked backward by the force of it.

"Betsie, hello!" Meg exclaimed, noticing that Josh hadn't dragged his eyes away from where he appeared to be having an intense conversation with Brin over by the row of old fishermen cottages.

"It's your party day! I saw the balloons outside!" The girl shrieked in Meg's ear just before she lowered her back to the ground.

"It is, I'm looking forward to seeing you later," Meg took the little hand which had automatically sought hers and began walking her back towards her father.

Hesitant to make her presence known to the man, but seeing no alternative, Meg plastered a smile on her face and hoped for the best. Clearly this was not good timing for an interruption, so she fully expected the grumpy bear to be the side of Josh's personality which greeted her.

Taking a deep breath she steeled herself.

TWENTY

It was plain to see the moment that Josh realised his daughter had eluded him once again, as his eyes flicked around him in a circle, suddenly oblivious to the older man who was still talking beside him, before turning his body so that he could scan the full area quickly.

"Betsie?" The word was out of his mouth before he caught sight of his daughter approaching with Meg, the woman who had punctuated his thoughts as he had sat up all night deliberating on what to do for the best, both professionally and personally. Then had come the text message from Brin asking him to meet here first thing, and Josh had been too intrigued to decline the offer, given as how it had simply mentioned a business proposition.

"Anyway, I'll leave you to think on it, lad," Brin said, tapping Josh's shoulder and heading back off towards the fish and chip shop, his gait a slow reflection of the years he had weathered.

"I've told you not to run off, poppet," Josh couldn't keep the exasperation from his voice as he crouched down to look directly at his daughter's face, "it frightens Daddy. The tide is out for now, but I've explained how when the water is close it would be very dangerous for you to get too near the edge."

"Sorry Daddy," the little girl's lower lip trembled and he scooped her into his arms, kissing her cheek and then whispering, "no harm done."

Meg smiled awkwardly and looked about to turn away, her duty of returning the little escapee discharged, so Josh grabbed her elbow gently to hold her in place.

"Sorry about last night," he whispered, as Betsie struggled to be put down so she could resume her shell-hunting of earlier.

"Nothing to apologise for," Meg said, watching as his

hand fell from her arm.

They both studied the girl poking in the sandy stones beside their feet, the silence for once uncomfortable between them.

"So, everything ready for the big day?" Josh asked, wanting desperately to finger the stray curl that had escaped Meg's scarf with one hand and to take hold of her hand with the other. Any physical contact, really, to appease his body which seemed to crave the woman's touch in whatever form he could get it.

"Yes, just came out for a bit of fresh air to, ah, escape myself really," Meg had no idea why she'd phrased it like that, inviting his further questioning.

"Oh?" Josh spoke the word as nonchalantly as possible, but inside he was desperate to hear the deeper meaning to her comment.

Had Meg spent the night thinking about him as much as he had tried not to think of her? Did it feel like her head and her heart were at odds too?

"I just mean I'm all set for the opening and can't stop myself tweaking things," Meg rushed out, hoping the half-hearted explanation would suffice.

"Look, Meg, I…" He began but Betsie's interruption

meant the rest of the sentence became lost amongst his daughter's happy squeals.

"Daddy! A rainbow shell," her chubby hand brandished the newly found treasure as if it were pirates' gold and both Josh and Meg immediately bent down to look.

"Beautiful," Meg admired the find.

"Really is," Josh agreed, though when Meg looked up she found him staring straight at her and not at the seashell. His eyes bored into hers, willing her to acknowledge the underlying meaning behind his comment.

"I, ah, should be getting back," Meg straightened up quickly, aware she was taking the coward's way out by refusing to own the attraction which was arcing between them like an electric current.

"Really?" Josh tried not to sound disappointed. It was her big day after all, and the offer he'd just received needed thinking over before he shared it with anyone. Still, the need to be close to her was a strong pull and Josh had to force himself to appear neutral. "Right you are, then, see you at twelve."

He watched as Meg bent down and said goodbye to

Betsie who threw her arms around the woman's neck for a hug, while Josh himself tried to tamp down the irrational jealousy that the action ignited. He berated himself silently for the ridiculous desire that he had been the one to hold Meg so close, to drink in the soft goodness of being so near to her, and tried to focus on the fact that it was so wholesome for Betsie to have a female role model who was neither her grandmother nor her aunt. Unfortunately, his body considered it little comfort and Josh wished his life wasn't so complicated – or at least that he would have the courage to follow his dreams and unravel it all.

However slowly the hands of the clock seem to turn, the time always comes. Meg had just finished reapplying her lipstick and ensuring Bonnie was safely shut in the flat upstairs, when the bell above the main door tinkled and the first of her guests arrived.

"Well, it said twelve on the invitation, but no one's here," the old woman spoke loudly and rather aggressively to the forty-something man pushing her wheelchair as if the lack of a crowd was his personal responsibility.

Although the space wasn't big, Meg was relieved she had made sure the shop was accessible to everyone and hurried to greet the pair.

"It's literally not even a minute past the hour, Mother."

"Well, at least we're first for free refreshments," the old woman snaked out a gnarly hand covered in knitted, fingerless gloves, and grabbed the top cupcake roughly from the display which Meg had painstakingly arranged earlier that morning.

"Hello, ah, thanks for coming," Meg said, watching almost horrified as the woman gobbled up the cake in two large bites before announcing loudly, "Awful, dry rubbish! Get me a glass of water, Edward, what're you waiting for?" Nevertheless, she was about to reach for another cake when the man in charge of her transportation swiftly moved her out of arm's reach of the baked goods and toward the small drinks table which carried a stack of paper cups, a jug of iced water and a matching one of lemonade.

Meg flashed him a smile of thanks as he extended his hand, "Edward Carruthers, pleased to meet you. My mother and I own the antiques shop at the top of the street."

"I own it Edward, not you, and don't you forget that,"

the woman interrupted before Meg could respond to his introductions.

Poor man, Meg thought, but aloud simply welcomed them to Brush Stroaks. The man himself blushed bright red at the admonishment and looked down at the floor in embarrassment. Thankfully, more guests began to arrive then, giving Meg a natural outlet from the awkward situation, until the small space was buzzing with chatter and conversation.

She felt him before she saw him, the hairs on her arms bristling and her body heating with an inexplicable awareness before Betsie came bounding up and cuddled Meg's legs from behind.

"You came!" Meg said happily, turning in the girl's embrace and smiling down at her in genuine pleasure.

"We did! Daddy had some boring things to do first," her frown of acute displeasure was almost comical, "are there any cakes left?"

"There are, but actually, I put this pink one behind the counter just for you," Meg busied herself, deliberately ignoring the feel of the man's eyes following her as she located the sweet treat and handed it to its eager recipient. Eventually though, she had no choice but to meet his hot gaze, drawn to him by the invisible string that seemingly refused to snap no matter how much Meg's brain told her to distance herself.

"It seems like it's going well, a huge success I'd say, all down to the gorgeous artist who brought this old place back to life," Josh whispered close to Meg's ear to be heard above the din. His closeness brought butterflies to her stomach, the fresh, salty smell of him testament to the fact he must've spent the best part of the morning outdoors. Josh's hair, too, appeared to have not seen a comb that day, and Meg's fingers itched to bring some order to the unruly locks. She let out a small sigh of longing, one which clearly hadn't been quiet enough as his cheek brushed hers then, his pinky finger finding hers in the small space between them and linking gently.

"It is," Meg replied, though she could barely remember what the topic was. His fingers rubbed against her hand in a rhythmic motion, that Meg would've been hypnotised by had the rude woman from earlier not made a loud commotion as she exited the shop, with neither a thank you nor indeed any word of acknowledgement in Meg's direction.

It was sufficient to break the spell, however, and Meg untangled her finger from his and moved behind the counter, her chest rising and falling noticeably with the depth of her breaths – somehow there didn't seem to be quite enough oxygen in the room despite the front door standing wide to welcome both guests and summer warmth into the old building.

Things had become more hectic after that, with a spillage in the children's corner to clean up, and a kind man from Upper Oakley who had purchased two paintings for his wife's upcoming sixtieth birthday. Those were the only sales of the day, though there had been interest in the art classes, and much excellent feedback to boost her.

All in all, the whole afternoon had left Meg happy and exhausted. Making a dream a reality was mostly hard work and adrenaline mixed with a small amount of exciting reward, and the opening of her shop was testament to that. Betsie and Josh had stayed for about an hour, but there had been no chance for any further closeness in that time, and in a way Meg had been glad of it. She had focused on her new neighbours – some of them hopefully future customers and students – and had been as mentally present as was possible. That had been important to her and Meg knew Josh would understand that.

Now, though, with the cleaning up finished and no one but a quickly growing kitten to keep her company,

Meg's thoughts drifted to the man she couldn't seem to get out of her head.

One thing was for certain, she either needed to take the leap or back away from the edge, because this state of longing was a distraction that Meg could ill afford. With a new business to run and the flat to renovate, Meg had enough on her plate already.

So why did she feel like a woman starved?

TWENTY-ONE

Almost two weeks passed.

Two long weeks in which neither Meg nor Josh made any move to see each other nor to communicate in any way, in fact. To be honest, Meg was also avoiding the tearoom and Janet's unsubtle queries as to when the pair were next going on a date. Her offers of babysitting were kind, but really only served to remind Meg that Josh had clearly made the decision for them both. To step away from the edge and onto safer ground. Clearly that also involved denying the other's existence, at least in the short term, as Meg assumed they'd both come to the conclusion that to be in one another's presence was too much of a temptation to act on the feelings that they couldn't seem to bury.

Out of sight had not been out of mind, however, as Meg's thoughts were determined to return to the tall man who had captured her attention in a way that no one before him had managed to do. Despite her concerted efforts – and better judgement – Meg couldn't help but wonder 'what if?'

What if they promised to be just friends? What if they agreed to taking things extremely slowly? What if they kept it a secret from everyone else? What if, what if, what if..?

It didn't help that she knew each weekday that Josh would be so close, just up the road dropping Betsie at Little Acorns. That he would no doubt be visiting his mum some days in the tearoom, right across the road.

What if she just happened to bump into him randomly one day?

It wasn't until a group of children came into the studio with their mothers to paint that Meg realised it was now the school summer holidays and Josh was likely in Upper Oakley most of the time, with no reason to bring Betsie into the lower village. Even that realisation, though, failed to stop her musings and Meg wondered if she should just bite the bullet and call the man. Just to get some sense of closure or whatever. To draw a firm line under the brief affair or whatever it had in fact been, and turn the page to a new, blank canvas.

Sometimes a masterpiece takes time, however, and is never quite finished until the artist decides, so Meg ended up making no move and was forced to live with the frustration of that decision.

Until today.

Today began unusually with a knock on the door and a bouquet bigger than the delivery driver's head being thrust into her unsuspecting arms. Meg hoped silently that it wasn't another of Chris's attempts at a reconciliation, though his silence since that one impromptu visit suggested he wasn't the sender. With trembling fingers which seemed to make the task much longer than it needed to be, Meg pulled the small card out of its envelope. A quick scan of the note brought a smile to her face and she rushed to find some paper to respond.

Dear Betsie, the flowers are beautiful and really did make me smile, thank you. Yes, I would love to come for tea with you and Daddy this Sunday at four o'clock. Love and hugs, Meg xx

That only left two days to decide what to wear.

And Meg's heart counted down every hour.

Josh rubbed his hands down his chino-clad thighs for the third time in as many minutes, wondering for the umpteenth time that day whether he was doing the right thing. His sweaty palms and brow might well indicate that this hadn't been a good idea, but then the thought of Meg always brought him out in a hot flush so it was frankly hard to tell. Either way, there was no going back now as the woman in question would be here at any minute.

"She's here! She's here!" Betsie jumped up and down in excitement as the sound of the doorbell chimed up the steep stairs into the flat. His daughter nearly went head first over a pile of boxes in her enthusiasm to reach the top landing from their small sitting room and Josh scooped her up just in time to avert possible injury.

That'd hardly be a good start, he thought to himself, *Betsie screaming the place down when Meg arrives.*

"You look so pretty!" Betsie greeted their guest with

gusto, grabbing hold of her hand and pulling her into their home, "Come with me upstairs, we have twirly pasta and a chocolate gat… gat… cake, and everything! The little girl barely paused for breath as she attempted to fill Meg in on the full two weeks since they'd seen each other.

Josh tramped up the staircase behind them. He had wanted to involve his daughter in this, to make sure what he offered was the full package, so to speak, yet now he was only minutes into the event and already wishing he had Meg to himself. Speaking of Meg, the summer dress she wore wafted lightly around her knees, hugging her behind so perfectly… Josh swallowed and dragged his eyes away.

This was going to be a long meal.

"Doesn't Meg look pretty?" Betsie returned full circle to her first comment as Josh indicated that their guest should take a seat on the sofa.

"Absolutely, definitely beautiful I'd say," Josh made eye contact with Meg for the first time in weeks and felt all of the pent up emotion and desire from that time release into his body. His chest certainly felt lighter, but other parts of him… well, didn't. Turning swiftly to stand behind the small table, which had had an extra chair added from the shed for the occasion,

Josh offered Meg a drink. Sadly, he only had soft drinks. He could've really done with some liquid courage right about now.

"A cup of tea would be lovely," Meg whispered, seeking his face out once again and smiling softly – nervously, Josh thought.

"Coming right up," he escaped to the kitchen, hearing his daughter launch into more of her 'news' as he put the kettle on.

"I've actually got something for you," Meg said, hoping to calm the little girl who was bouncing between sofa and armchair at a dizzying rate.

"Oh?" Betsie did indeed pause, before eying Meg's large canvas bag which rested on the floor beside the woman's feet.

"I do, if that's okay with Daddy?" It was an afterthought and Meg really wished she'd checked with Josh before she offered the gift. She really wasn't used to children and the nuances of how things should be approached.

Josh was just walking into the room and thankfully nodded his approval, "Of course, though if it's edible, maybe best to keep for after…"

"No, no," Meg reassured him, "just something I saw on a visit to Alnwick yesterday."

She pulled the squishy offering from her bag, still with tag attached and was unable to provide any more clarification before she was drowned out by the shrill squeal of the gift's small recipient.

"It's Billy Bear! Daddy, do you see? It's a Billy Bear just for me! He is for me, isn't he? I don't have to give him to Little Acorns?"

"He is absolutely for you," Meg handed the toy to the little girl, who hugged it straight to her chest, the sight all the thanks Meg needed.

Betsie suitably distracted, Josh offered his hand to Meg. No second thoughts needed, she placed her slightly smaller hand in his and allowed herself to be pulled to her feet and into the circle of his embrace.

"Thank you," Josh whispered into her hair, taking a deep breath in of the scent of roses that always seemed to surround her. It invaded his senses and made him almost lightheaded.

Or maybe that was just the proximity after what had felt like ages apart?

"Thank you for the invitation," Meg said, hoping they

would have some time later to discuss exactly what she was being invited to. A meal? A friendship? A place by his side and in his be…

Meg shook her head slightly to clear the image and focused back on the small girl who had returned from her bedroom with her arms full of other toys, ready to introduce them to her newest, softest arrival.

Squeezing her hand silently, Josh retreated back to the kitchen whilst Meg tried to remember the onslaught of toy names she was furnished with. Now squashed on the sofa with Betsie and her array of cuddlies, the cosy moment brought a lump to Meg's throat for reasons she didn't want to let herself explore. Whether it was her own grief for her aunt, little Meg's desperate wish for a mother, or grown up Meg's inner yearning for a family to call her own, it was all she could do to blink the tears away in time for tea.

TWENTY-TWO

"You didn't need to do that," Josh spoke as Meg entered the room, closing the door to Betsie's bedroom slowly so as not to wake the infant.

"I know, but I loved that story when I was little, it was my pleasure to read it to her."

Thankfully four year olds go to bed relatively early, so the evening was still young. Meg followed Josh's extended arm and came to sit with him on the sofa, that and the dining table being the only spaces that didn't seem to be encroached on by boxes.

"Are you, ah, leaving?" Meg asked. It had only

dawned on her that the flat was all but packed up and ready to move once they had all settled at the table for their meal and Meg had had enough of a breather from Betsie's attentions to scan the room properly. Ever since then, a small ball of worry had nestled in her stomach and she couldn't wait any longer to ask the question which was the source of her discomfort.

Had he invited her here to say goodbye? Had encouraging the man to follow his dreams ironically been the thing which took him from her? Meg wasn't sure she could hear it – and surely it would be cruel to Betsie to encourage a relationship tonight which he knew had no future – and yet she had to know…

"What? Oh! The boxes, yes that was one of the things I wanted to tell you about."

Meg cast her eyes immediately downward so that he wouldn't see the hurt and disappointment there.

"Hey, let me explain," Josh immediately took Meg's hand in his, using his other index finger to tip her chin gently back so as to establish eye contact once more, "Betsie's already unsettled about the move, so I didn't want to mention it when she was in here, but I see now that was a mistake. I've caused you undue confusion and, ah, well, we are moving but only down to the harbour."

"The harbour?" Meg parroted back, embarrassed by the squeak that her voice had become.

"Yes, turns out my mam had been filling Brin in on my predicament and he knew that old Charlie Russell had up and sold his fishing boat and was looking to sell his cottage and workshop down there too so he could move down to Hartlepool to be with his son. For once everything fell into place at the right time, as Joy who runs the florists here in Upper Oakley wanted a bigger property where she could add a bookshop and café. My mam's not overly keen about the café part, but since it was the missing piece I needed to get my finances squared and start again…" Josh paused, realising suddenly that he was simply firing information at Meg now.

"I'm really happy for you," Meg whispered, "really happy." Which she was, but still wondered if this had somehow just been a celebration of that good news and…

"So of course that led me to think of you, well, everything leads to thoughts of you," Josh bumbled on, hoping he wasn't making a complete pig's ear of this yet suspecting he certainly was.

"Really?" They seemed to be taking turns at interrupting each other, but neither seemed to mind as

Meg gave his hand a little squeeze to encourage him to keep sharing.

"Yes, Meg, yes, I know I'm in the middle of a lot of upheaval, and I'll have to spend a lot of time reassuring Betsie and getting her settled at the new place, not to mention the work it needs to modernise the cottage…"

"We could do that together, though."

"We could. I was hoping you'd say that. I just couldn't wait for the perfect time to begin something between us and risk losing you to someone else. When does the perfect time ever come anyway? Life always throws up curveballs."

"It does, and the more pairs of hands to help catch them the better," Meg said, before realising she sounded very cheesy and feeling her face heat up.

"Exactly, so Betsie and me, we're starting afresh. I'm following my dream to be a joiner and carpenter, the new place has a workshop and it's close to my sister, I should've said all this sooner, I just needed to get it all sorted first. Especially since you're the one who encouraged me to follow my dreams… But I was wondering if, if you'd, I mean how you'd feel about…" He had practised this all week, but now that the moment was here Josh found his mouth dry and his mind blank, not to mention he was staring at Meg's lips like a parched man eyes water in the desert.

Meg decided to put him out of his misery, leaning forward slowly to close the gap between them until her mouth was mere centimetres from his, "Are you saying you'd like to build a relationship with me Mr. Carter? Something that hopefully goes beyond friendship?" She knew she was teasing him, breathing the words out in a husky whisper.

"Yes, that's exactly what I'm say…" Josh began as Meg's mouth landed on his and silenced the rest of the sentence with a kiss.

Josh had spent the past few minutes in the tiny bathroom in his flat splashing his face and arms with cold water. Things had heated up faster than he'd intended and when Meg had pulled back – albeit clearly reluctantly – and suggested she start clearing up while he checked on Betsie, he had taken the opportunity to cool off a bit despite knowing full well there was nothing for her to do in the kitchen as he'd done the washing up while Meg had been telling his daughter a bedtime story. It wasn't appropriate to get hot and heavy on the couch while his child lay in the room next door, and Josh was thankful that Meg shared that opinion.

Opening her door a crack and seeing Betsie's face in the half light spilling into her room from the lounge, her features cherubic in slumber and as if carved from smooth planes of glass, Josh was reminded of another carving he had meant to deliver this evening. Turning into his own bedroom before joining Meg in the kitchen, he retrieved the wooden piece from the drawer of his bedside table. No bigger than the size of his palm, it was what the gift represented that Josh hoped would add gravitas to its small stature.

"I made us a cuppa since you'd already sorted the plates and pans," Meg said, handing him a mug of tea and taking the opportunity to add a small peck to Josh's cheek.

"Thank you, I actually have something for you too," Josh guided them both back to the sofa, shoved aside a box to place both their mugs on the coffee table, and then perched beside Meg, nerves assailing him now that the moment had come.

Would she think the gift stupid? Too forward or, worse still, inappropriate in some way?

Too late, she looked at him now expectantly, her legs resting over his as if they had always shared evenings this way, in companiable cosiness, and Josh had the sudden desire that things always remain so easy and comfortable between them.

"I, ah, it's just something small…" he handed it over without further ado, blushing and turning his face away to hide his nerves.

"It's The Tree! Did you make this?" Meg strove to keep her excitement in check so as not to wake Betsie, turning the wooden object over and over in her hands as she sought out each tiny detail.

"I did," he still couldn't look at her.

"It's perfect, Josh, really, the proportions, the angles of the branches. Wow, really, thank you. It must've taken you ages."

"It was something to distract my hands while I thought of you," Josh felt his blush deepen, realising the way his words had sounded, "sorry, that wasn't intended to sound crass, I meant…"

"I know, I know, I'm just so touched, thank you," it was Meg's turn to tip his face towards hers now as she peppered soft kisses along Josh's forehead, down his temple, over his cheekbone and finally arriving at his lips to whisper, "it's perfect."

"I know what it means to you, The Tree," Josh said eventually, his breathing heavy and his voice gruffer and deeper than usual, "how special the place is. I hope in the future it can be a special place for both of us."

"It already is," Meg said, the happiness in her heart reflected in her face, "it's Our Tree now."

TWENTY-THREE

A month had passed in a blur, filled with working in Brush Stroaks during the day and unpacking boxes and redecorating Betsie's new bedroom in the small cottage by the harbour in the evening. Meg had agreed with Josh that the other rooms could wait until the little girl was settled in her new space. The couple had been careful not to be too affectionate, not too physical in front of his daughter, to give Betsie time to get used to having Meg around a bit more. When the infant was in bed, though, well that was a different story altogether, and the weeks had given the fledgling relationship a passion-filled boost.

"It's okay to still think about her," Meg said one teatime as she worked on the final corner of the mural she'd been painting on the wall opposite Betsie's bed.

"I know," Josh picked up the framed picture that always sat on his daughter's bedside table, of Claire looking worn out and beautiful holding a tiny baby Betsie in the labour ward, "it's hard though. I feel guilty for my anger after her death. I can see now that dreams are inherently selfish, that's the nature of them. But to stop someone pursuing their heart's desires, well that's maybe even more so. We were in a tug of war where no one was ever going to win."

"I'm glad you can think of her more kindly now, that's only ever a good thing. She'll always have a part of your heart, Josh, and that's exactly as it should be."

"I can only understand these things better because of you, Meg, because of what you've shown me. Yes, Claire will always be a part of me, but so are you now. Nothing is ever as black and white as I used to see it – thankfully I get that now."

Meg put down her paintbrush and crossed the short distance between them, wrapping her arms around Josh's waist from behind. He replaced the photo gently and turned to face her, his eyes glassy.

"I'm so grateful for you," he whispered.

"And I for you," Meg replied, tilting her head to accept his kiss as her eyes fluttered closed.

"We're ba-ack," two voices called in unison, one an excited child and the other her grandmother sending a warning to the two lovebirds in the adjoining room. To say Janet had been excited about the new relationship would be a considerable understatement. Indeed, the woman had gone out of her way to give Josh and Meg as much peace and privacy that first month as possible. Today she had opted to take Betsie shopping for the flower girl dress that she would wear the following weekend for Josh's best friend's wedding.

"Look Meg, look Daddy, it's got flowers on it, and a little pocket in the front. I wonder if my Billy Bear will fit in there?" As fast as she had entered, Betsie whirled off to her bedroom to find the toy in question, twirling her new frock about her head as she ran.

"Careful not to get it dirty," Janet called after her, and to Josh said, "I doubt the bear will fit in that tiny pocket, so there may be some tears before bedtime."

"No worries, Mam, thanks for taking her."

"Get a lot done, did you? Make a lot of progress?" She added a wink to the question and Meg felt her cheeks heating.

"Mam!" Josh said, "Yes, the mural's almost finished. Oh! Mind the wet paint in there, poppet!"

Meg smiled at the hubbub of family life as Josh went to retrieve the new dress and hang it somewhere safe from little fingers. It really was joyfully imperfect.

It was as they were all sitting around the new farmhouse kitchen table – one of several pieces of furniture Josh had found in a local house clearance sale to tide them over until he could make his own pieces for the home – that Janet's face suddenly clouded over while they discussed the logistics of the following Saturday. Who would drive whom and the like.

"Is everything okay, Janet?" Meg asked, always attuned to dips in mood after walking on eggshells around her father for so many years.

"Well, ah, I'm not sure she'd want me telling you both this, but I'm worried and I've said everything I can to persuade her… Jenna is determined to miss the wedding. Which would be fine, except The Oakettes are the main entertainment at the reception up at the hotel."

"Well, she'll just have to put on her big girl pants and get through it," Josh said, before clocking Meg's slight frown at his harsh response and immediately tempering his tone, "it's been, what? Ten years? Twelve? I know Nick left and broke her heart, but they were kids, barely eighteen. Surely she can't still be pining after him?"

"Maybe it's because he was her first love, or perhaps just that the heart wants what the heart wants, but you know she's never found anyone she wants to be with for more than a few months since then." Janet shook her head sadly.

"Is he married now? Out of bounds?" Meg asked, not knowing any of the backstory.

"No, I see his mam in Upper Oakley occasionally and she doesn't talk of him much, but I get the impression Nick is far from settling down and making a home with anyone. Not that he's been back to Oakley from what she says. No, he simply left for the army and disappeared from our Jenna's life never to return. Unfortunately he apparently set the bar so high it seems no one else will do," Janet sighed heavily and took a gulp of her tea.

"That's hard," Meg agreed, "though it does sound doubtful he'll show up at the wedding himself, especially since you say he hasn't been back since he left that first time."

"Well, he and Simon and I were best friends," Josh said, "me and Simon initially at primary school, but after that Nick tagged along a lot, especially after he started seeing Jenna our final year of high school. If Simon's managed to get hold of him, which I'm pretty sure he mentioned he had, then I reckon Nick'll come. Never was one to shirk what he considered a duty."

"Can you try to talk to your sister then, lad?" Janet asked, the hope clear in her eyes.

Josh looked at his mother like she'd just asked him to wrestle a tiger in his undies with only a baking tray as protection, "Since when did she listen to me?"

Janet sighed and nodded, leaving Meg wondering what would happen at the wedding if both Nick and Jenna did show up.

TWENTY-FOUR

"You look beautiful. Stunning, in fact," Josh's eyes were out on stalks as Meg did a small twirl in the doorway of the art shop, her fifties-style, floral dress flowing out from where it was cinched in tightly at her waist. He and Betsie were here to collect her to go to the wedding together, earlier than the other guests, so Betsie could have a final practice of her flower girl duties and Josh could begin his as best man. The little girl in question was currently bouncing up and down like the Easter rabbit, complete with empty wicker basket with ribbons woven around its handle, her tight curls barely moving in the slight breeze.

"Well thank you, kind sir, you're not looking too

shabby yourself!" Meg drank in the sight of him, all clean shaven and scrubbed up in a suit and tie as she took Josh's offered arm and allowed the pair to lead her to the car. They were taking her own, rather clapped out mode of transportation today, as even in its somewhat decrepit state the car was cleaner and more suitable for their smart attire than Josh's work van.

"Did Jenna head over there earlier to practice with the band?" Meg whispered as the car groaned to life under her feet.

"Well, she tried to call off sick yesterday, but my mam texted to say that Robyn from the tavern came down last night and apparently talked some sense into her. Or at least promised a united front with the other two Oakettes if Nick does show. Hopefully she feels less alone now. I mean, she has us and my mam and Brin, but no amount of family can stop you from that kind of loneliness, you know?" Josh spoke from the heart of experience.

"Oh I really do," Meg agreed, "also, I got the impression when I first arrived that Robyn and Matt were a couple. Since they're not, I imagine Robyn herself knows a lot about feeling lonely despite having company most of the time."

"Absolutely, now that's a pair that needs a kick up the a…" Josh suddenly remembered his daughter in the back seat, "a shove in the right direction, if ever there was one." His thumb moved in slow circles over her knee, Meg's legs bare in the warm weather, sending a shiver of awareness right up her spine.

Controlling her reaction, Meg simply nodded and joined Betsie in waving to The Tree as they passed, her special place glowing in the morning sun and fully cloaked in its summer foliage.

It was a much chillier scene, doused in shadows, as the couple drove down to the old oak at dusk that day. High on the love and romance of the occasion, Meg had eagerly agreed to Josh's suggestion that they sneak out for a short while and visit their favourite spot whilst Betsie was showing off her moves on the dance floor with Janet and Brin. As Meg hadn't drunk anything alcoholic, happily being the designated driver, there was nothing to stop them from running off, giggling like schoolchildren playing hooky.

"Is someone else here?" Meg asked nervously, her tone laced with sudden disappointment as they approached the tree, seeing an unusual green plastic sticking out from behind.

"Hold on, I'll check," Josh let go of her hand and tiptoed around, "no, just a sleeping bag and a backpack. Guess someone's forgotten them or is planning a night under the stars. Either way, no one's here to disturb us now." He didn't give the out-of-place, abandoned objects another thought as he went back to join his love, who was already placing her palms against the cool of the wide trunk.

"So, are you going to tell me what you wished for now?" Josh whispered, only half serious as he knew Meg liked to keep it a secret.

"Actually, yes," she replied, "I have a new wish now, so I see no harm in telling you my old one."

Josh relaxed back against the bark and pulled her close, flat against him as he breathed in the floral smell of her, "If you're sure? I was just joking."

"I am," Meg lay her palms flat on his chest, feeling the smooth suit jacket and itching to slip her fingers inside to feel his skin's warmth through his shirt, "I used to wish for someone to share my dreams with. Now I have that, I have you." She swallowed down the lump in her throat and smiled up at him through unshed, happy tears.

"Funny that, because that time we came here and I made my own wish, I hoped for someone to give me permission to follow mine. My dreams that is. In the end, I realised only I could do that for myself. Though a certain beautiful artist did give me a push in the right direction!" He rubbed the tip of his nose against hers before peppering kisses over her face until Meg giggled with the ticklish sensation.

Meg felt the warmth of his words as their bodies began to sway together in the new moonlight. A slow dance of heady love and tightly controlled passion which brought every nerve ending to life and overwhelmed her senses in the best possible way. His soft kisses and gentle caresses, the beauty of the day they'd shared, the promise of many more to come… It was a precious time Meg would never forget.

She turned briefly to the ancient oak tree and smiled widely as her body moved to nature's rhythm and her breaths matched those of the beautiful man in her arms, grateful for the dreams that had brought her to this moment.

"I love you," Josh whispered, his forehead now tipped to rest against her own.

"I love you too," Meg replied, cupping his cheeks with both hands, "my dream come true."

EPILOGUE

Jenna tried hard to remember the words to Ella Fitzgerald's 'I've Got A Feeling I'm Falling,' aware of the small beads of sweat that graced her brow and upper lip. Despite having sung the song many times with her '40s tribute group, The Oakettes, today the lyrics and harmonies eluded her. Her band sisters covered for her, of course, carrying the performance and making up for her own faltering act. Something Jenna wasn't proud of, but needs must.

The irony of the song's title hadn't passed her by either, as what with the nausea and headache, Jenna did indeed feel as if she were falling. Not only that, but her 'wartime chic' dress felt too clingy, too itchy and scratchy to be comfortable today, her heels too high, her hairgrips pulling against her scalp and fighting with her copious amounts of hairspray in a way they normally did not.

She knew the reason, of course. The heightening of her senses, her hyper-awareness was not by chance. No. It had everything to do with him, Nick Drummond, the man nonchalantly sitting at the bar as if he hadn't a care in the world. Jenna had promised herself she wouldn't let the sight of him affect her, would keep her furtive glances in check and certainly wouldn't keep looking to make sure he was still where she last saw him all of two minutes ago. Her body, however, had other ideas. She was like a moth to a flame and the constant internal struggle of trying to pretend he wasn't there whilst simultaneously wanting to drink him in was taking its toll.

As soon as the song was finished, thankfully the last of that set, Jenna excused herself to hurry to the bathroom, hoping to give herself a firm talking to whilst she dabbed at the wet droplets that she hoped hadn't smudged her makeup. Unfortunately, by the time she'd sat in a stall and finally given in to the tears that had threatened all day, there were a lot more wet blotches to deal with and still a final set of love songs to get through on stage. One of her most-used phrases as a preschool teacher in Little Acorns, 'We can do hard things,' came into her mind to tease Jenna as she patted face powder over her cheeks from a small vintage compact in a desperate – and rather futile attempt – to hide the evidence of her upset.

Head down to avoid any neighbours who might want a chat, Jenna escaped the ladies room without meeting anyone she knew. Taking a deep breath of relief, she walked straight into a wall. No, not a wall, as it hadn't been there earlier. *A person?* Jenna allowed her eyes to creep slowly upwards, old black boots, shined to within an inch of their lives, dark suit trousers pulled taut over thick thighs that seemed to go on forever… she skipped over the rest of the torso quickly, the sinking feeling in her stomach growing with each second that passed. Though, to be honest, it felt as if time stood still, so great was her embarrassment and reluctance to make eye contact.

"Hello Jenna," the gravelly voice was lower than she remembered, but none the less recognisable. It had visited her in her dreams often enough over the years to never be completely gone from memory.

Her eyes finally met his, blue to brown, as Jenna felt she might faint from the heat and the battering of her heart in her chest, as if like a bird it might want to escape its cage altogether.

How embarrassing it would be if she did actually…

"Jenna, hold on I've got you," Nick felt the panic burst in his chest, the familiar swell of anxiety that quickly exploded if he didn't practice the techniques he'd been taught over months of therapy. There was no time for them right now, though, nothing to do but to push past the crowds and out the side door of the hotel into the cool night air, cradling his precious cargo. He hadn't meant to shock her so badly. After all, they'd both been aware of the other from the first moment his body had recognised her presence in the church. She had been sitting two rows behind him and almost out of his line of sight even if he turned and craned his neck, but nevertheless he had sensed she was there then and every moment since. Like the painkillers in his pocket he'd tried not to take all day, she was a constant pull he could never quite shake off.

Of course, that desperate wanting had faded over the years, had become buried under camaraderie and then pain and guilt, to the point that Nick had genuinely wondered if he'd even recognise her now. Well, there's no bigger fool than a fool in love. Of course he had recognised her and not just that, his body had remembered. How she looked, how she felt, how she sounded when they were together. There was no way he was getting through today without just once being close enough to study her properly. How time had matured her face, how her girlish figure had filled out. He had finally decided to allow himself this one time, this one close encounter before he returned the borrowed suit to Simon and headed back to his makeshift bed for the night. And look what had happened.

"What..?" Her voice was shaky as she came around, her body pressed against his chest suddenly lighter as she began to carry her own weight and quickly lifted her head off him. Nick felt the loss of her warmth as much as he felt the guilt that it had been him who had caused Jenna to black out in the first place. He carefully lowered her down onto her feet, holding her arm to steady her until her balance returned fully.

"I'm sorry," the first two words out of his mouth then were probably the most weighted ones he could have chosen, but Nick didn't have time to plan a second speech. The one he'd spent all day rehearsing in his head had been binned the moment Jenna collapsed so it was all pot luck from here on in. Not ideal for a man who liked to be in control, who was always prepared, who said nothing if there was nothing worthwhile to say.

"No, I was just hot, not been sleeping well. I've been on my feet all day, no time to eat…" she swayed slightly and inadvertently rested against his chest again.

Nick wasn't entirely sure Jenna realised who she was talking to. Sure enough, as if she suddenly became fully aware of him, a moment later saw her pulling away in a desperate hurry to break the contact. Not just moving off him, Jenna actually took several quick steps backwards to put a decent amount of space and air between them.

"Nick," the word escaped her dry lips on a whisper, her hand shooting out to grab the railings of the car park wall to steady herself.

"Jenna, I'm so… I didn't mean to give you a fright. Let me get you a glass of water, something from the buffet, you just wait here, I'll…"

"No!" The whisper had become a shout, "No, I can look after myself, thank you."

And with that she was gone, back into the hotel and out of his arms and his life once more.

Was this how she had felt when he left her all those years ago? So bereft, as if the air had been sucked out of her lungs all at once?

Nick bent double, the force of the feeling akin to being kicked in the stomach.

"Too much to drink, eh drummer boy?" Some old school mates jibed at him as they passed. People he hadn't seen for over twelve years, and really had had no intention of ever reacquainting with.

Well, let them think he was drunk, it was better than feigning an interest in each other's lives anyway. For sure, Nick had done more small talking today than he had in all the intervening years.

He kept his head down and tried to control his breathing, count of three in, hold for four, five out. Rinse and repeat. He ran his sweaty palms over his freshly washed hair and simply focused on the air entering and leaving his body. His body which he could, to some extent, control. These panic attacks, the desire to outrun his skin as if that were a thing, these were a usual part of his life and his body now. But his mind? That was a different matter entirely. His brain couldn't forget the feel of her in his arms again after all this time, the homely smell of something clean and floral. *Lavender?* He didn't know enough about flowers to know for sure. One thing Nick did know though, was that he was grateful Jenna had seen him at his best. He would never have allowed himself to take advantage of the groom's hospitality by accepting the offer of a room for the night in the hotel, but he had availed himself of a shower that morning. Heaven forbid she saw the state he normally lived in.

With that thought, and the complex range of emotions it brought up that had Nick throwing up into the nearest rubbish bin, he decided he'd done enough revisiting his past in this one day to last a lifetime. From the confrontation with his mother first thing to the botched attempt to catch up with Jenna now, the whole event had simply reinforced in Nick what he already knew.

What he had always known.

He did not belong in Oakley.

Can the hurts of the past make way for hope in the future and new, happy memories to be made?
Or are these two lonely souls destined to never find a home with each other?

Read Nick and Jenna's story next in "Making Memories on Oak Tree Lane."

R. A. Hutchins

Making Memories on Oak Tree Lane

Oak Tree Lane Book Two

Publication Date March 15ᵗʰ 2024

Take a stroll down Oak Tree Lane, the home of cosy community and healing hearts.

Jenna has always known exactly where she belongs, right here in Lower Oakley. By day a preschool teacher in Little Acorns, by night part of a 1940s tribute quartet known as The Oakettes, Jenna has never felt the desire to spread her wings further than the small Northumberland village where she grew up.

Nick has never felt like he belonged – neither in Upper Oakley as a child, nor in the army as an adult. The British Armed Forces provided a temporary base, but since his recent medical discharge Nick has been bouncing from one hostel to the next, unable to put down any roots.

In fact, the only time in his life that Nick ever felt at home was during his brief relationship with Jenna

when they were eighteen. High school sweethearts
who ultimately wanted different things, the pair have
deliberately not seen each other since their painful
break-up.

Until now.

Strange things can happen on Oak Tree Lane, though,
where second chances can make old love new.

Can the hurts of the past make way for hope in the
future and new, happy memories to be made?
Or are these two lonely souls destined to never find a
home with each other? A new mystery series from R. A.
Hutchins, author of the popular Baker's Rise Mysteries,
combines the charm of a Yorkshire seaside town with
the many secrets held by its inhabitants to produce a
delightful, cosy page-turner.

ABOUT THE AUTHOR

Rachel Hutchins lives in northeast England with her husband, three children and their dog Boudicca. She loves writing both mysteries and romances, and enjoys reading these genres too! Her favourite place is walking along the local coastline, with a coffee and some cake!

You can connect with via her website at: www.authorrachelhutchins.com

Alternatively, she has social media pages on:

Facebook: www.facebook.com/rahutchinsauthor

Instagram: www.instagram.com/ra_hutchins_author

R. A. Hutchins

OTHER ROMANCE BOOKS BY R. A. HUTCHINS

The Angel and the Wolf

What do a beautiful recluse, a well-trained husky, and a middle-aged biker have in common?
Find out in this poignant story of love and hope!

When Isaac meets the Angel and her Wolf, he's unsure whether he's in Hell or Heaven.
Worse still, he can't remember taking that final step.
They say that calm follows the storm, but will that be the case for Isaac?

Fate has led him to her door,
Will she have the courage to let him in?

To Catch A Feather
Found in Fife Book One

When tragedy strikes an already vulnerable Kate Winters, she retreats into herself, broken and beaten. Existing rather than living, she makes a journey North to try to find herself, or maybe just looking for some sort of closure.

Cameron McAllister has known his own share of grief

and love lost. His son, Josh, is now his only priority. In his forties and running a small coffee shop in a tiny Scottish fishing village, Cal knows he is unlikely to find love again.

When the two meet and sparks fly, can they overcome their past losses and move on towards a shared future, or are the memories which haunt them still too real?

Read on for an excerpt...

These books, as well as others by Rachel, can be found on Amazon worldwide in e-book and paperback formats, as well as free to read on Kindle Unlimited.

AN EXCERPT OF *TO CATCH A FEATHER*

Kate sat back against the smooth, weather-beaten stone and let the wind rush over her, drying her tears just as quickly as more fell to replace them. She looked out over the North Sea, grey and foreboding on this cold February day. It was welcoming in its bleak anger, the waves whipping up and over the pier below. She had seen it in all its moods, this natural beauty, from the turquoise peace of a summer's day to the most violent of storms, crashing against the rocks below. Here, from the shelter of the ancient priory at her back, she was merely an observer to its rage. And yet it set her free. Free from the emotions which tormented her thoughts. Free from the guilt of tasks incomplete. And more. Most importantly, free from the suffocation of sitting with her own thoughts at home.

Home. Kate wasn't sure where that was any more. Was it the small flat she shared with her best friend, Sal? Was it back with her parents in their 1960s bungalow? Or with her church family, on one of her increasingly infrequent visits to Sunday services? Kate sighed as the thoughts flitted through her head, an image of each place providing a fleeting question. None gave the answer she desired. Then there was Patrick – Rick to those who knew him well – his image hung longer than the others. His boyish grin and freckles. His unruly hair. Kate managed a small smile. The face of the man she was to marry never failed to give her a momentary feeling of warmth, of happiness perhaps.

Happiness. Another illusive notion. Kate couldn't remember the last time she had felt joy. Real, jump up and down and clap your hands wildly joy. The kind that bubbles up without restraint and infects all those around you. She had tried of course, but it was like catching a feather on the breeze. Illusive. Kate tried to think back to the last time she had registered the emotion. Any emotion, in fact, other than numb resignation or acute despair. The only moment that had come close was when Rick had proposed at her surprise thirtieth birthday party last August. She had been happy, then, hadn't she? Kate couldn't be sure. Not because the question hadn't pleased her, not because she hadn't said yes immediately, but rather because she seemed incapable of feeling happiness, even at one of the most important moments of her life. Rick had grinned with relief, taking her in his arms and kissing her passionately. Her parents had been excited at the prospect of seeing her wed, and of course her friends had begun speaking of wedding preparations excitedly. But Kate. Kate had kissed Rick back, nodded and smiled at everyone else, allowing inspection of her beautiful ring to fill the spaces where conversation should have flowed. In private later that night, she had prayed for God to release the hold of the anxiety and depression which held her heart in their claws. Her personal demons, Kate had battled them for most of her life. At times they were like old friends, annoyingly familiar and requesting her attention. At other times, like this past year, they became harsh taskmasters, directing her thoughts and actions, dictating her responses and her emotions. Kate felt like a puppet in their game.

She ran her hands through her windswept curls distractedly, pulling her scarf tighter about her face and sighed audibly. There was no one else here on this bitterly cold day, and Kate fished in the pockets of her woollen coat for the gloves she kept there. She was meeting Rick in an hour and needed to pull herself together. Wiping her nose and eyes ineffectually on her very damp tissue, Kate watched a seagull dipping and diving out on the waves far below. *How would it feel?* she wondered. *How would it feel to be set free, to just go away and ride whatever waves came her way?* The prospect was not an unattractive one, and Kate deliberately chose not to pursue the thought further. It would do no good, and would only serve to upset her further. The chains that trapped her were internal, not external. Where she ran, they would too, adding weight to her every step. No, Kate would meet Rick shortly in their favourite coffee shop, she would go to work tomorrow morning, in the vet's surgery where she was a nurse, and neither her fiancé nor her colleagues would be any the wiser to her personal torment.

Rick hovered at the top of the main street, beside the large, ornate fountain, wringing his hands. He knew that Kate would be there already, waiting patiently at their usual table, a cup of mint tea in front of her, teabag still in the cup. He knew her, what she liked to drink, her favourite books and music, even how her freshly-washed hair smelt. And yet, here he was, feeling as if he were about to meet a stranger. Increasingly indifferent to life and to him, Kate didn't seem to be bothered whether they met up or not these days. Between the start of the year and now, the couple had seen each other only three times. When Rick stopped initiating their dates, he had found that Kate made no comment. She didn't share any suggestions of her own, didn't text to say she was missing him. Nothing. If anything, she had shrunk further into her shell.

Not wanting to live together until married, Rick had hoped that their intimacy might increase at least a little after their engagement. More times spent getting to know each other in private rather than at the cinema or in restaurants. But, if anything, the opposite had been true. Kate had even declined to spend Christmas with him and his family back in Ireland. And that had been the final straw. So now he trudged with heavy feet and a heavier heart, along to meet his fiancée. The last time he could probably think of her as that, Rick noted morosely.

The heat of the small café hit him as he walked in, adding to his not inconsiderable discomfort. Rick ordered his usual caramel latte and headed to the far corner, where Kate sat observing him whilst blowing the steam from her cup. Her red curls were in disarray and Rick swallowed the lump that had formed in his throat at the sight of her.

"Hey," Kate said, half-standing to accept his peck on the cheek.

"Hey, you," Rick replied, shrugging out of his winter

coat and taking the chair opposite. "How's it going?" He noted her swollen, blotchy face but made no comment.

"Oh, fine," Kate gave her stock answer, "You?"

Rick could hardly bare the pleasantries. He had better conversations with his aged aunt. As his coffee arrived, and the owner, Dan, provided a brief distraction, Rick decided that blunt was best.

"So, Katie," he said, using the term of endearment that he had created for her early in their relationship, then immediately regretting it, "I guess we need to talk." It was unoriginal, he knew, but he had nothing else, nothing better to lead with.

Kate's ears pricked up at that. His tone, his demeanour, were different from the easy-going man she was used to. Her heart began to beat a funeral chant in her chest. Kate had been here before. Not engaged, but her previous long-term boyfriend, Chris, had broken up with her after three years, stating he wanted to travel. He'd moved as far as York and taken up with the worship leader at his new church there. Within the year they were married and expecting their first child. What he'd meant by 'travel', Kate had deduced, was to get away from her. From her melancholy. Looking up into the eyes that were so familiar, yet so distant, Kate braced herself for the worst.

"How do you feel things are going? With us, I mean?" Rick rushed the sentence, keen to begin the conversation and reach its inevitable conclusion.

"How do you feel things are?" Kate expertly turned the question back to him. She was adept at avoidance.

"Well, I, I'm…" Rick struggled to find the words, realising too late that he should have practised this more. Written it out and learnt it by heart, perhaps. But even the thought of saying it, had grieved him such that he'd put it off till this moment. "I'm not feeling so close to you anymore." *Had he ever?* Rick wondered silently. There, he'd said it. Well, not quite said it, but it was a start.

"Oh?" Kate looked back at him enquiringly, her head tilted to one side, her face masking the inner turmoil which made her feel as if she were about to vomit.

She said nothing further, and Rick was forced to expand. Sighing heavily, he reached across to where her hands cradled her cup, and took one between his own, larger palms. "When we first met," he began cautiously, "things were great, weren't they? We met up a few times a week for dates, we talked for hours in this very coffee shop. We… shared things. Our hopes, our lives." He paused and looked Kate straight in the eye. It was she who turned away first. "But over the past six months, since we got engaged, you've become... distant." He raised an eyebrow speculatively, expecting a response. A denial. Anything.

They sat in awkward silence for seconds which stretched into minutes. Finally, pulling her hand out of his, Kate spoke in a whisper, "Say it, Rick, say it and put us both out of this misery!"

Rick swallowed the emotion coiled in his throat. Did he really want to do this? Once spoken, the words could not be unsaid. He looked into the watery green eyes of the woman he loved. The woman he still loved.

Kate returned his gaze, wishing she could explain that her anxiety, held in check until last Summer by a combination of medication and CBT strategies, had been sent into overdrive as a result of a natural flare-up and then the pressure of others' expectations. His included. Talk of setting a date, making huge life choices, had weighed heavily on her mind and her chest until she was suffocated. Her doctor had suggested a change in regime, and the new prescription had, of course, come with side effects – Kate felt numb most of the time, to her anxiety, yes, but it was so much more than that. She was desensitized to life itself. When she wasn't distant and unreachable, even to herself, she was filled with an anguish so acute, it felt like a storm raging inside her, drowning all rational thought. She would not inflict herself on others, and so had retreated from friends and fiancé alike.

"I love you." Rick's whispered words released the flow which had barely been held in check up to this point, and Kate could not help herself. The tears streamed down her face. His hands found hers again and squeezed gently, Rick's thumbs rubbing a path around her palm. "I love you." He said it louder this time, his eyes never leaving hers.

"I love you, too," Kate whispered, seeing his shoulders visibly relax as he heard the truth in her words.

"Thank you," Rick could think of nothing else to say. It was what he had needed to hear. That she was not indifferent to him. It was a start. "Listen, Katie, let's not think of the wedding anymore."

"You want to break off the engagement?"

"What? No! I'm just saying that we need to shift our focus for a bit. To us. The two of us. Together."

"Oh, okay." Kate scrubbed at her wet cheeks with her free hand. Rick took his hands back and they both took a moment to regroup, sipping their drinks thoughtfully.

"Let's go away," Rick began, having clearly come to a decision, the determination etched now in his sombre expression. "Away?"

"It's half term in two weeks, I don't have much marking or preparation to do. Let's go away!" Rick held his breath, watching as Kate's thoughts flitted across her features.

"But we aren't married!" she whispered.

"Oh, come on, Katie! We're not in Victorian England, your reputation isn't at stake! We can get separate rooms if it'll make you feel better!" He tried, and failed, to not let his exasperation show.

"I do have a lot of holiday days accrued…" Kate began to think seriously about the prospect. Perhaps a change of scene would do her good? Somewhere in the countryside? She nodded and smiled. A real smile. The first in a long time.

one's cup of tea and that's ok because I prefer a skinny chai tea latte. I wasn't put on this journey to be liked by all and everyone's best friend. My journey has taught me that life really is short and that it is so important to be able to call out those who behave in ways that are just not right. It may be that they behave in this way because this is all they know and have seen. However, what would be worse would be to not tell them when their behaviour is wrong.

We all have a journey to take, many winding roads, traffic lights and the occasional brick wall to climb over. I want you to all know that you can do this. Sometimes you may need some support and most of the time if you just stop and breathe you will find a way yourself.

It is so important to be true to yourself

> *"Never be afraid to raise your voice for honesty, truth and compassion against injustice, lying and greed. If people all over the world did this it would change the earth."*
>
> — *WILLIAM FAULKNER*

We are almost at the end of my chapter and I do hope that you have enjoyed everything you have read and maybe even been inspired to go out and live your dreams. Here are a few questions that I would love for you to consider when you have a moment.

How did you feel about your own journey as you went through my journey with me? Ponder over this when sitting alone reminiscing about life with your cup of tea or coffee

How would you have reacted if that had been you or you had seen this happening to someone you knew?

What changes can you make to empower yourself, your family, friends and colleagues so they do not have to go through this in their lifetime and for those after?

Who should you share this story with to inspire them to know the road may be hard but they can succeed?

It would be so wrong if I did not take a moment to mention my husband, Dhani, our two children of the four-legged kind, Neo and Ri, my father and my brother Jayesh, who each day inspire me, make me laugh and support me to do the things I want to do that make me happy.

I'd like to raise a glass of champagne and say Thank You, Thank You, Thank You, to all those people who made my life difficult, who created noise when it was unnecessary, who chose their own egos over showing kindness, put up barriers at each step, and tried to make me feel even smaller. You have helped me to become who I am today. A better person with more understanding and a drive to inspire, change and succeed in life.

So, who am I?

I am an Award-Winning Celebrant, Toastmaster and Public Speaking Expert and I am awesome.

Be Kind.......

Dare to Dream, Dare to be Different

The World is Your Stage

Sonal Dave

Ms Sonal Dave

ABOUT THE AUTHOR

Sonal Dave

Sonal Dave has led an exciting and eclectic career and is now bringing her passions together as an Award-Winning Ceremonies Celebrant, Toastmaster and Public Speaking Expert.

Sonal Dave has been flagged as a 'name to know' in the events industry. She has already won the hearts of many, won awards and been featured in many publications. She is also excited to share that her Communicating with Confidence workshops and online courses have CPD accreditation.